The Old Ladies

HUGH WALPOLE

Books by HUGH WALPOLE

NOVELS

THE OLD LADIES
THE WOODEN HORSE
THE GODS AND MR. PERRIN
THE DARK FOREST
THE SECRET CITY
THE CATHEDRAL

The London Novels

FORTITUDE
THE DUCHESS OF WREXE
THE GREEN MIRROR
THE CAPTIVES
THE YOUNG ENCHANTED

Phantases

MARADICK AT FORTY
THE PRELUDE TO ADVENTURE

BOOKS ABOUT CHILDREN

THE GOLDEN SCARECROW
JEREMY
JEREMY AND HAMLET

BELLES-LETTRES

JOSEPH CONRAD: A CRITICAL STUDY

The Old Ladies

By

HUGH WALPOLE

The pathetic story of three old gentlewomen who lived at the top of a creaky, rickety
house. In their characterization Mr. Walpole por-
trays with poignant realism and loneliness of old
age reduced to penury and want. An exceptional
study in human values.

39106

NEW YORK
GEORGE H. DORAN COMPANY

PR
6045
A34
O4

THE OLD LADIES

— A —

To

ETHEL

WHOSE GOODNESS TO THE WEAK
THE AGED AND THE LONELY
IS AS UNOBTRUSIVE AS IT IS MAGNIFICENT

"The old ladies were soon forgotten in the pursuit of more exciting personal ties . . . They sat in a row, deserted."

HENRY GALLEON.

CONTENTS

CHAPTER   PAGE

I Mrs. Amorest Pays a Visit 13

II Evening in the House—Agatha Payne 37

III Life of May Beringer 58

IV Red Amber 79

V Christmas Eve — Polchester Winter Piece 108

VI Agatha Secretly 137

VII Death of Hopes 159

VIII May Beringer Tries to Escape . . . 182

IX The Sense of Danger 210

X Death of May Beringer 234

XI Mrs. Amorest Shows Courage . . . 259

XII The House Is Abandoned 283

THE OLD LADIES

THE OLD LADIES

CHAPTER I

MRS. AMOREST PAYS A VISIT

QUITE a number of years ago there was an old rickety building on the rock above Seatown in Polchester, and it was one of a number in an old grass-grown square known as Pontippy Square.

In this house at one time or another lived three old ladies, Mrs. Amorest, Miss May Beringer, and Mrs. Agatha Payne. They were really old ladies, because at the time of these events Mrs. Amorest was seventy-one, Miss Beringer seventy-three, and Mrs. Payne seventy. Mrs. Amorest and Mrs. Payne were wonderfully strong women for their age, but Miss Beringer felt her back a good deal.

It was a windy, creaky, rain-bitten dwelling-place for three old ladies. Mrs. Payne lived in it always; although she had fine health her legs

were weak and would suddenly desert her.
What she hated above anything else in life was
that she should be ludicrous to people, and the
thought that one day she might tumble down in
Polchester High Street, there in front of everybody, determined her seclusion. She was a
proud and severe woman was Mrs. Payne.

Mrs. Amorest and Mrs. Payne had lived in
these rooms for some time. Miss Beringer was
quite a newcomer—so new a comer in fact that
the other two ladies had not as yet seen her. The
lodgers on that top floor of the house had the
same charwoman, Mrs. Bloxam, and she came
in at eight in the morning, cooked the three
breakfasts, stayed until ten and tidied the rooms.
After ten o'clock the three old ladies were
alone on their floor of the house, very nearly
alone indeed in the whole building, because the
second floor had been a store for furniture but
was now deserted, and the ground floor was the
offices of a strange religious sect known as the
"Fortified Christians." The only "Fortified
Christian" ever seen was a pale dirty young
man with a blue chin who sometimes unlocked
a grimy door, sat down at a grimier table, and
wrote letters. Mrs. Amorest had once met him

in the ground-floor passage, and it had been like meeting a ghost.

Mrs. Amorest herself stayed indoors a good deal, because three pair of stairs were a great number for an old lady, however strong she might be.

She looked an old lady of course with her snow-white hair, her charming wrinkled face, and her neat compact little body. She had also eyes as bright as the sea with the sun on it, and a smile both radiant and confiding. But she was like many other English old ladies, I suppose. I suppose so, because she never attracted the least attention in Polchester when she walked about. Nobody said, "Why, there goes a charming old lady!"

She had never known a day's illness in her life. When she had borne her son, Brand, she had been up and about within a week of his birth. And yet she had none of that aggressive good health that is so customary with physically triumphant people. She never thought about it as indeed she very seldom thought about herself at all.

Another thing that one must tell about Mrs. Amorest is that she was very poor. Very poor indeed, and of course she would not have lived in that draughty uncomfortable room at the top of the old house had it not been so.

She liked comfort and pretty things, and she had been well acquainted with both when her husband had been alive. Her husband, Ambrose Amorest, had been a poet, a poet-dramatist ("Tintagel," A Drama in Five Acts, Elden Foster, 1880; and "The Slandered Queen," A Drama in Five Acts, Elden Foster, 1883, were his two best-known plays). For a while things had gone well with them. Amorest had inherited from his father. Then quite suddenly he had died from double pneumonia, and it had been found that he had left nothing at all behind him save manuscripts and debts. A common affair. Every novel dealing with poets tells the same story. Brand, the only child, had at the age of eighteen gone off to seek his fortune in America. For a while things had gone well with him, then silence. It was now three years since Mrs. Amorest had heard from him.

Indeed, the old lady was now very thoroughly alone in the world. Her only relation living was her cousin Francis Bulling, who also lived in Polchester. It was because of him, in the

first place, that she had come to Polchester; she
thought that it would be like home to be near
a relation, the only one she had. But it had
not been very much like home. Mrs. Bulling
had not liked her; and even after Mrs. Bulling's
death, when Cousin Francis had been a grim old
man, sixty-eight years of age, tortured with gout
and all alone in his grim old house, he had not
wanted to see her.

He was rich, but he had never given her a
penny; and then, one day, when she came to
see him (she never thought of the money but
felt it her duty occasionally to do so), he had
laughed and asked her what she would do with
twenty thousand pounds a year.

She had said that she did not know what she
would do, and he had said that he might as
well leave it to her as to any one else. She had
tried not to think of this, but money was the
one power that forced her sometimes to think
of herself. She had so very little, and it was
dwindling and dwindling because, kind Mr.
Agnew her solicitor explained to her, her investments weren't paying as well as they did. She
knew very little about investments. Her view
of money in general was that one must never

get into debt. She paid for everything as she got it, and if she couldn't afford something there and then, she didn't get it. From quarter to quarter the sum had to stretch itself out, and kind Mr. Neilson at the Bank wanted it to stretch, she was sure, as far as it could, but, powerful man though he was, he couldn't work miracles.

Although she thought every one kind and most people nice she was not a fool. She was not blind to people's faults, but she selected their virtues instead. She felt that she was an old woman with nothing interesting, amusing, or unusual about her, and therefore did feel it very obliging of any one to take an interest in her. It could not truthfully be said that many people did. She had her pride, and she did not like her friends to see her poverty, and so she did not ask them to her room. On the other hand, she did not wish to accept hospitality without returning it.

Then, even though you are very strong, if you are over seventy and a woman, you have only a limited store of energy. Mrs. Amorest was often weary, and sometimes felt that she COULD not face THOSE STAIRS!

In her dreams at night the stairs figured, long-toothed, dragon-scaled, fiery to the foot—her demons!

But when she had reached her room, then all was well. In these years she had grown fond of that room. Once, when investments had behaved more nobly and she could ask her friends to visit her, it had been a very gay room indeed. She had always liked pretty things, and had inherited from her earlier, more prosperous married life certain fine pieces of furniture. In the right-hand corner of the room was her bed, and in front of the bed a screen of old rose-coloured silk. There were three old chairs also fashioned in rose colour, a rug of a rich red brown, a little gate-legged table, and on her wash-hand stand her jug and basin were of glass, and the little water jug had around it a wreath of briar-rose. She had, too, a bookcase with twelve volumes of *Macmillan's Magazine*, some stories by Grace Aguilar and Mrs. Craik, and Tennyson's complete works in eight volumes; also the four books published by her husband, one of poems and three of plays.

Her chiefest treasures were on her mantelpiece, a faded photograph of Brand aged twelve in football clothes—"such a sturdy little chap" was the phrase she had used in the old days when there had been visitors—and a drawing of her husband, a thin figure with hair flowing, a cape flung over his right shoulder and a book held prominently in the hand. "A rather weak face" that same visitor might have thought, but to Mrs. Amorest, rich in intimate memories, perfection; perfect in physical beauty, in spiritual significance, in human sympathy.

The room was a large one, and might seem to the superficial observer chill and spare. The chest of drawers and the cupboard where Mrs. Amorest kept her clothes could not cover sufficiently the farther wall space. The windows were not large. Mrs. Payne had the view right over the Pol and the country beyond. Mrs. Amorest had chimney-pots and not a glimpse of the Cathedral. Miss Beringer had the Cathedral, but her room was a pound a year more than Mrs. Amorest's.

Mrs. Amorest would not have a fire until the winter had really quite closed in, and the difficult days were such as these in November when it could be so cold and so wet and so wild and yet it was not truly winter. To-day was not a bad day; a pale ghostly light was over the world, the sky was scattered with tatters of white cloud as though for a celestial paper-chase, and the smoke from all the chimneys blew wildly in the wind.

Mrs. Amorest noticed these things as she prepared to go out. The Cathedral had struck (very faintly heard from here) two o'clock, the sun suddenly made a struggle and threw a faint primrose glow upon the remains of Mrs. Amorest's little luncheon—a coffee cup, a tumbler, a plate with crumbled biscuit, and a half-empty sardine tin. Three water biscuits, one sardine, and a cup of coffee, and Mrs. Amorest felt fortified for the rather difficult visit to her Cousin Francis that she was about to pay.

As she arranged her bonnet over her beautiful white hair in front of the misted looking-glass she was suddenly aware that she was going to like this visit to her cousin less than any that she had ever paid him. She would like it less for two reasons; one that he was very ill, and that she would therefore be in the hands of his housekeeper, Miss Greenacre, who both disliked and despised her; the other that kind Mr. Neilson had written to her to tell her that there were only Ten Pounds Four Shillings and Fivepence to her credit in the bank, and Quarter Day was yet far distant, and that therefore the thought of Cousin Francis's money was more dominant in her brain than it had ever been before.

She didn't wish it to be so. As she stood there, twisting the purple strings of her bonnet in her thin beautiful fingers, she thought how wicked she must be to have this in her mind!

But as you grew older you seemed to have less and less power to keep things out of your mind. You were being punished perhaps for looseness of thought in your earlier days. You had been too happy and careless then and must pay now. It was the one remnant of Mrs. Amorest's strict puritan upbringing that she felt that God did not intend His servants to be too consciously happy. And yet with her, all her life, happiness would keep breaking in. Probably she must pay for that now.

She gave a little sigh as she turned away from the window. She was still wickedly hungry. That was the punishment for being physically so blooming, that you had always so healthy an appetite. She looked for a moment covetously at the sardine tin. One more sardine, one more biscuit. Then resolutely shook her head, and as was her way often when she was alone her face

broke into smiles.   How ridiculous to have such
an appetite with her small body!   Now if she
had been Mrs. Payne . . . !

And perhaps if she were in a kindly mood Miss
Greenacre would offer her some tea with some
of those nice sponge fingers that Cousin Francis
had.   She was not really greedy, but she liked
sponge fingers.

Before she went out she listened for a moment,
her head cocked on one side like an enquiring
bird.   How silent the house was!   Like a dead-
house.   The wind was playing through it like a
musician plucking a note from a board there, a
stair here, an ill-fitting window somewhere else.
But the house itself gave no sound.

Mrs. Payne too—how silent she was!   There
in her room day after day, thinking, thinking—
of what?   Of her past, one must suppose.   After
seventy the past was of so much more importance
than the present.   And the new tenant, Miss
Beringer, how quiet she was!   She had been there
for three days now and Mrs. Amorest had not
yet seen her.   "A nice-spoken lady," Mrs. Bloxam
had said, "and fond of talking."   Tall and thin
and dressed in pale green, a strange costume for
one of her years.   And having decided this with

a thought of cheerful approbation for her own grey silk, Mrs. Amorest started down the stairs.

Cousin Francis lived in a large stone house on the other side of the river. It was shortest if you dropped down into Seatown, crossed the wooden bridge by the mill and walked through the fields, but Mrs. Amorest avoided Seatown when she could. She hated to see the distress and poverty that she could do nothing to improve; and although a stout optimistic lady had once told her confidently that "the poor were always happy. They had none of the troubles that weighed on the rich" she couldn't altogether believe it. They had none of the *same* troubles certainly, but she herself had known for too long what it was to worry about every penny, and deny yourself everything comfortable and easy, to believe eagerly in poverty.

So to avoid Seatown she crossed the Market-place and the bottom of the High Street and turned to the left over Tontine Bridge, skirted the river for a little way and then climbed the wooded path to Cousin Francis's large white gates.

She was tired and weary and anxious to-day. Do what she would she could not beat down her

anxiety. Passing through the streets as unob-
trusively as possible, she would nevertheless have
rejoiced had there been only somebody to raise
a hat or smile a smile. There was nobody at all;
she mattered to nobody. In that whole town
there was not a soul who cared whether she lived
or died, and realising that in the sharp November
wind she gave a little shiver. Her legs ached
to-day and her brain ached. That particular ache
in the brain came directly from her effort to keep
her thoughts in order and to bring them into some
sort of consecutive discipline. Her thoughts to-
day were like mice behind the wainscoting—tap
tap, scratch scratch—there for a moment and
then gone. Some stockings that must be mended;
a discolouration of Mrs. Bloxam's eye that, said
Mrs. Bloxam, had been caused by tripping over
a coal-scuttle, but was derived, Mrs. Amorest
feared, straight from Mr. Bloxam's fist; strange
Mrs. Payne with her old discoloured purple velvet and her bushy eyebrows; and there go Mrs.
Combermere and Miss Ellen Stiles! How strong
and self-confident they look! Mrs. Amorest had
not been always a shy woman. In those days in
Cheltenham when Mr. Harland and Mr. Crack-
anthorpe had come to stay over Sunday, she had

acted hostess bravely, although she could never like the things that they liked, thought the books that they read and wrote quite horrible if the truth be known. Her husband had never been able to change her artistic tastes. But she had not shrunk from Mr. Harland, had indeed chaffed him a little, but now were Mrs. Combermere to stay and speak to her she would tremble all over and stammer most-like, and have no words of her own! And yet how happy she would have been! What an event in her day! Once, at a party at the Dean's, she had been introduced to Mrs. Combermere. But that seemed long ago. The time for parties at the Dean's was past and gone; for one thing she had no clothes, for another some one might one day call on her and spy out the nakedness of the land, for another. . . .

She shivered again as she crossed the Tontine Bridge.

Then she beat up her spirits. What was happening to her? How unlike her to lose her courage! It must be that tiresome Ten Pounds Four Shillings and Fivepence that was worrying her. Never mind that. She had been in worse troubles than that ere now and God the Father had always come to her aid. He would come to her aid again. As she looked up to the cloud-streaked sky, a sky into which a faint orange glow was slowly stealing, she felt, as on so many thousands of occasions she had felt before, the presence of a large protecting friend Who put His arm out towards her and drew her up, and smiling said, "How could you ever have doubted . . . ?"

Nevertheless she doubted once again as she walked up Cousin Francis's grim and desolate drive. Cousin Francis had that property, peculiar to certain natures, of bestowing the colour of his personality on everything and everybody close to him. His garden, the rooms of his house, his housekeeper, his secretary, his Irish terrier, his two gardeners, all of them were wind-bitten and desolate. With all his money he did not know what comfort was, nor colour, nor gentleness, nor the "laughter and the love of friends." His own gaunt and rocky body with its high cold forehead, its naked eyes and projecting teeth, its long legs and iron-grey hands held no comfort for any human soul. Even his dog did not care for him.

The house was like a gaol with its barricaded windows and cold ugly walls. Mrs. Amorest pealed the iron bell and then waited, her heart beating beneath her thin grey silk. There was a fine view of Polchester from here, the Cathedral riding triumphantly on high, the houses and fields piled up at its feet, and now suddenly the sun burst its bonds and great swaths of golden glory enwrapped the scene. Mrs. Amorest stood entranced and did not hear the door open and the voice of the maid.

She turned and, blushing, said, "Oh, I beg your pardon. How is Mr. Bulling to-day?"

"A little better, mum."

"Oh, I'm glad of that! I wonder if I might see him for a moment?"

"If you'll step in, mum, I'll enquire."

Mrs. Amorest stepped in and was left alone in the large stone hall with its empty fireplace, its grim portrait of Mr. Bulling as Mayor of Drymouth, and its shining wooden chairs.

She looked very small in that high cold place, and Miss Greenacre, Mr. Bulling's housekeeper, might be forgiven perhaps for looking all about her for quite a while before she saw that there was anybody there. Miss Greenacre was long and thin and white and ribbed like a stick of asparagus. She had the air of one who has so many important things in mind that personal contact with her must be always three times removed. And especially for Mrs. Amorest she was removed into almost disappearing distance.

Having found her, she only said "Good afternoon," biting her words as she offered them as though to see whether they rang true or no.

"I came to enquire after Mr. Bulling," said Mrs. Amorest. She was often timid with Miss Greenacre. How fervently she wished that she was not, and the more fervently she wished it the more timid she was.

"I wonder whether I might see him for a moment?"

"Well now, that depends," said Miss Greenacre, looking down upon Mrs. Amorest with a considering air as though she were a colour waiting to be matched.

"He wasn't so well this morning, but since he's had his dinner—well, he's brightened up considerable."

Mrs. Amorest might be timid, but she refused to be patronised by any one.

"I wonder whether you would mind," she said quite sharply, "letting him know that I am here?"

Miss Greenacre entered into the game with steely zest.

"Do you know, I believe he's just dropped off —about five minutes back. It wouldn't be well to wake him, would it?"

"I think he would like to see me," said Mrs. Amorest. "If you wouldn't mind making sure whether he's asleep or not."

"Well now . . . I wonder. . . ."

She stood there biting her finger and considering. Mrs. Amorest had a sudden burning ambition to pick up a large bronze of Neptune near the door and hurl it at her. Would she then snap in two or bend? The thought of her surprise made a little smile hover about Mrs. Amorest's lips. She got up.

"Would you mind," she said very firmly indeed, "asking whether Mr. Bulling will see me?"

And to her great surprise Miss Greenacre suddenly turned and went.

Alone once more, Mrs. Amorest abruptly sat down again. She was more weary than she had known. Her legs now really were *not* strong. That walk had exhausted her more than it had ever done before, and a sudden fear, confronting her not for the first time, whispered to her that the day was coming when she would be like Mrs. Payne—alone up there at the top of that silent house forgotten by all the world, slowly more helpless, more lonely, more——

She bit her lip because her chin trembled. Her chin was always giving her away. It seemed the least stable part of all her anatomy.

"Miss Greenacre shan't see that I'm worried," was her thought, and Miss Greenacre did not, returning just then to say that Mr. Bulling was awake and would see Mrs. Amorest.

Up the heavy oak staircase the two women went, through passages that glimmered under the guttering gas with bad oil paintings of heavy seas and buttercup meadows, and so into the long high bedroom, dark and close and smelling of medicine.

Mrs. Amorest had often visited her cousin in bed before, and was accustomed to the shining forehead, the long cold nose, the pale bony hands. Propped up against his pillows, he peered out at her like a large malevolent bird. His bed was canopied with heavy dark red curtains. On the table beside the bed was a lamp with a green shade and a row of medicine bottles. Mrs. Amorest, coming forward, noticed none of these things in her sudden discovery that he had changed terribly for the worse since her last sight of him.

Her heart was touched: the maternal was roused in her. He was suffering, and there was no one really to care for him. That horrible Miss Greenacre could not be called anything. How uncomfortable he looked! She longed to turn the pillows, to smooth the sheets, to turn the shade so that the light was not in his eyes! But even with that impulse she realised that Miss Greenacre, watching her, would say to herself, "Ah, there goes another after his money!" And was it not true? Only on her way to this house . . . So the impulse was checked and she stood there in her purple bonnet and grey silk, smiling a little, and at last timidly saying:

"And how are you, Cousin Francis, to-day?"

"Worse; that's the way I am," he growled from the bed; then raising his voice, "All right, Greenacre. You can leave us. I know you'd like to overhear every word we're going to say, but you can listen behind the keyhole and you won't hear a thing."

How terrible, thought Mrs. Amorest, to treat any one like that and to call her "Greenacre."

Could I ever endure it, she wondered, if I were in that position? No, indeed, I could not. But the lady did not appear discomforted. She gave Mrs. Amorest one haughty glance and departed.

"Sit down, sit down, Cousin Lucy. And take off your bonnet. I like to see your hair." This last remark was in a softer tone. It encouraged Mrs. Amorest, who took off her bonnet and laid it on the table near the medicine bottles, then brought a chair and sat down close to the bed.

"Come to see how the poor old man's getting along? To see how fast he's dying and when his money's going to be divided?"

Mrs. Amorest's pale cheeks flushed. "It wouldn't be true, Cousin Francis," she said, "to say that I haven't thought about your money, because I have, and reproached myself for doing so. But I haven't thought greatly about it, and I would have come to visit you if you hadn't a penny in the world. I would have come indeed more often than I have done."

"Well, that's honest," he answered. "More honest than most of them. I'm glad you've come to-day. It's probably the last time you'll see me."

"I hope indeed not."

"But indeed it is. I'm dying, and I'm frightened of it. I've been a man all my life that's never needed anybody. I never needed a woman or a friend. My mind was given to the making of money and I made it, and now it seems a shame that I can't take any of it with me. Sometimes, when the pain's bad, I want it all to end as quickly as may be, but when the pain goes, there I am again thinking of the money and wondering how I can make the most of it in the little time that's left. But I'm lonely, Cousin Lucy, mighty lonely. All my life I never thought to be, but that is the truth now I'm here. I'm lonely and naked at the last."

Mrs. Amorest said what she could, but her mind was fixed on the desire to arrange his pillow, to smooth his hair from his forehead, to do something that would make him comfortable. His long cold fingers kept plucking at the sheets, his eyes were never still. But she would not do anything lest he should think that she wanted his money.

"What would you say to it if I were to leave you a thousand pounds a year?" he asked her.

"I should be thankful to you," she answered him. "I have not many years to live, but I would find out my boy and we could live together again."

"Where is your boy?"

"I don't know." Against her will tears gathered in her eyes. "I haven't heard now for a considerable time."

"Aye, he's forgotten you, I've no doubt. So you're all alone?"

"Yes, I'm quite alone."

"It must have tired you coming up here to see me?"

"Yes, it was tiring."

"How old are you now?"

"I was seventy-one last March."

"Were you now? We're both old dodderers. Are you afraid of death?"

"No, Cousin Francis."

"And why not?"

"My Heavenly Father will care for me in that as He has cared for me in everything else."

"Cared for you, you say, when He has left you all alone in your old age?"

"I am not alone while He is with me."

"Well, I don't understand all that religious nonsense. But what if it should be true, after all? Who can tell? Nobody knows."

There was a silence between them, a long silence. Then the man said:

"You're a good woman, Cousin Lucy—the best of all of them that come here. I'll give you a thousand pounds a year. On my oath, I will. I'll see Agnew about it to-morrow."

Mrs. Amorest turned very pale. Then she said faintly: "Thank you, Cousin Francis."

"Is that all you've got to say? I like that too. You're not a false one like the others. Let me feel your hair."

She came closer to the bed, and he put his hand on her white hair and very slowly stroked it. They sat for a long time, he stroking her hair. Then suddenly his hand fell away and she saw that he was asleep.

She gently put on her bonnet and stole out of the room.

CHAPTER II

DARKNESS gathers swiftly in November, and below the rock the lights of the Seatown slum gaily flickered. There came up to the black walls of the houses some shadow of the last pale afterglow of the sunset, and motion was sent spinning through the evening air by the shrill, discordant notes of a cornet that some one in Seatown was enjoying.

In Pontippy Square there was no life. The tides of Polchester had passed it by. The old houses once, in eighteenth-century years, fashionable and alive, had sunk their chins into their breasts and so slept. Used largely once for warehouses, they were now, like No. 19 where lived the old ladies, let out in pieces to occasional lodgers. It was the shabbiest inch of all the genteel districts of the town.

In the Square there were only two lamps, and these at opposite corners, so that the space before

No. 19 was unlighted. The pavement here, too, was broken and grass-grown so that it made a splendid trap for the unwary. After dusk, to navigate the holes and broken stones, then to find the door, to turn the round iron knob, to discover the stair-rail, and then successfully to start upwards into the forbidding dark, was no mean feat of seamanship, and, for an old lady, it was dangerous indeed.

Some years before an old lodger had been discovered by the milkman in the morning at the bottom of the stairs with her neck and many bones broken. She had fallen a full flight. She haunted, poor old wispy-haired crumpled lady, the Square after dusk. She always had with her a little sniffing dog. You could feel him sniffing at your trousers or skirts.

The silence of Pontippy Square was another matter of note. The sniffing of a ghostly little dog could indeed be heard miles away if you chose to listen for the sound. But silent though the Square might be, once within the house with the heavy old door closed behind you, and you sank deep, deep into a well of oblivion. You might climb the stair with the hope perhaps of discovering it livelier if you went higher. But the silence follows you. When, out of breath, on the third floor now, you pause and listen, it is only the hammering of your heart that you hear. Silence everywhere.

Mrs. Payne's room was the first on the right of the stairs. If you opened the door and looked in after dusk (a liberty very rarely taken by any one), the first things that you noticed were the two big red candlesticks and a large piece of faded orange silk hanging over a cupboard opposite the door. It was a large room and curiously jumbled with odds and ends. On the round table there was a sewing basket of pink silk, a china dish with oranges, a black-haired doll in a green dress, and two packs of cards scattered on the shabby red table-cloth. The candles in the red candlesticks gave but a faint light, and you must look well before you saw in addition to a bed a chest of drawers and the cupboard with the orange silk across it, a large black rocking-chair, a cuckoo clock, and a big oil painting of an aquarium scene—a very large picture this, with green shining water and large fish with open mouths. There was also a stuffed bird with crimson wings in a glass case.

After these things, your eyes now accustomed

to the uncertain light, you perceived their mistress. Mrs. Payne was a large, stout, and shapeless woman. She had hair of a deep black and her cheeks were highly coloured. She had fine dark eyes. She looked an old gipsy woman, and perhaps she had gipsy blood in her—foreign blood, for sure. She would be rocking herself in her chair, lying back in it wearing her soiled red wrapper and her shabby crimson shoes. She was not a cleanly old woman. Her splendid hair, as black now as forty years ago, was tumbled about her head carelessly, and stuck into it, askew, was a cheap black comb studded with glass diamonds. Her colour was swarthy, brown under the deep red of her cheeks, and there was a faint moustache on her upper lip. But she must have been handsome once, a fine bold girl in those years long ago. Quite shapeless now, her fat dirty arms naked under the wrapper, her body as it lolled back in the chair boneless. Once and again she yawned, then felt in a dirty paper bag on the table near to her for a thick slab of nougat that she crumbled idly in the bag, then ate fragments, licking slowly her fingers. Her face was expressionless. Her large black eyes stared out into the room vacantly.

As she licked her fingers she kicked one foot idly in the air. But she was not vacant. She knew what she was about. When the cuckoo burst his little door and cried that it was seven o'clock she would rise, totter across to the cupboard, produce a plate, a cup, a loaf of bread, butter, jam. She would make herself a cup of thick rich cocoa (the kettle had been long on the fire), and she would eat many pieces of thick bread and raspberry jam, and then a hunk of black dark plum-cake.

She would eat sitting up at the table, staring in front of her, her lips making a large smacking sound of satisfaction. Then once again she would lick her fingers slowly, elaborately. Then once again totter back to her chair, lie on it and rock, tossing her shabby red shoes in air.

Totter! Yes, because the only sign of age was in those legs of hers. They alone had deserted her. They would betray her in a moment, the knees failing, and she must cling to the table to save herself from falling. She hated her legs—they had betrayed her—and in the dark recesses of her mind she would imagine how she might punish them, punish them without hurting herself, just as though they were separate personalities.

But on the whoie she was not ill-contented, nor did she bear humanity a grudge. She did not dislike this life of hers. She had always been lazy, taking what came nonchalantly. She had taken Wilfred Payne and his miserable mother; she had taken a lover and his brutal desertion of her; she had taken a child that had not been her husband's (and he had never known); she had taken its death; she had taken the Roman Catholic religion for the lights and the incense; she had taken her husband's death and her own subsequent poverty; she had taken the job of companion to an old fool widow of a Polchester merchant; she had taken the widow's decease (without leaving her a farthing) and her own subsequent penury; she had taken Pontippy Square and the cold and silent room there; she had taken her absolute loneliness and isolation—everything she had taken with a luxurious sensual indifference. Her two passions—and they were in their basis one—were for food and bright colours.

For food her longing was both active and indolent. Active because she would take trouble that Mrs. Bloxam should keep her well supplied in cake and jam and nougat. She spent all that she had on these foods, and in her slothful brain there was a kind of wonder that she could purchase so much of this for so little. Her digestion did not apparently suffer.

Her passion for bright colours was a deeper longing. It had always been so. As a tiny child she had cried after a reel of coloured thread and had begged for a shining marble. And this had gathered strength perhaps because her husband and mother-in-law had sternly forbidden it. Theirs was the Nonconformist mind and vision: grey stone, drab clothes, uncoloured minds. She had hated her husband for many reasons, but chiefly because he had thrown a gay hat of hers into the fire. She would lie in bed beside him devising tortures for his soft and rounded limbs. But that was many years ago. She had long forgotten him. The past appeared to her a succession of bright and shining images. Her husband was not one of these. She did not think connectedly of her past at all. Old people do not. To the old the past comes in a series of pictures, not of necessity connected, here intensely vivid, there dim and blurred—a green field, a quiet evening, an angry quarrel, some loving face, some sharp disappointment—and all, vivid or blurred, dispassionately removed. No call for action any more. Quiescence. And then a strange wonder that to those about them these scenes so real, so actual, mean nothing, stir no reaction.

But Mrs. Payne did not wonder. She had no audience for her memories; only Mrs. Amorest who seemed to her a silly old thing, incredibly old, stupidly active, an egoist in her sense of her importance.

With this matter of activity Agatha Payne was always intending to be "on the move" one day soon. Nothing forced her to stir. Her monthly allowance was paid to her by a lawyer in Birmingham. He paid her rental for her room. The rest was in Mrs. Bloxam's hands, and Mrs. Bloxham might cheat her if she willed, so long as she brought her what she desired.

But Mrs. Bloxam did not cheat her. She had a strange tenderness towards her two old ladies. When, before the arrival of Miss Beringer, there had been two old ladies and one old gentleman, she had been yet more tender towards the old gentleman, and were there now three old gentle-men her tenderness would have known no

bounds. She *did* prefer the other sex and always
had. But, as she said to Mr. Bloxam, you
couldn't help but be sorry for the two old things.
She liked Mrs. Amorest the better of the two;
there was something in Mrs. Payne's lazy indifference that frightened her, and then "her liking
sweet things the way she did." Like a child.
But then if it hadn't been sweet things it would
have been drink, and *that*, as Mrs. Bloxam only
too absolutely knew, was "another kettle of fish."
Mrs. Bloxam, too, was honoured by Mrs. Payne's
trust in her, and would take real trouble over
the commissions she gave her, going "quite a
way" up the High Street to find the raspberry
jam that she preferred. But whereas Mrs.
Amorest was a "real sweet old lady," and should
have been "a Duchess in her own right if all had
their proper due," Mrs. Payne was "not quite.
. . Well, you know. Shouldn't wonder if she
went queer in the 'ead any day."

Mr. Bloxam, when he was sober enough to
realise things, couldn't see what Mrs. Bloxam
was about wasting her time with those old women.
It wasn't as though she got anything for it—
but Mrs. Bloxam felt like a mother to them,
twenty years younger though she was. She felt,

too, a certain power. She liked to see Mrs.
Amorest's eager smile when she called her in the
morning, and to feel Mrs. Payne's dependence on
her. "If they 'adn't got me surely to goodness
I don't know who they would 'ave and that's the
truth. Poor old dears."

About Miss Beringer she had not as yet made
up her mind. Miss Beringer had been there but
a week. And then there was the fox-terrier.
"Pip." A silly name for a dog.

It was not to be expected that Mrs. Payne
considered Mrs. Bloxam as a separate identity.
Had Mrs. Bloxam been a stick of nougat or a
piece of brightly coloured silk then Mrs. Payne
would have desired to possess her, and her sluggish brain would have suddenly awakened to the
intention of possessing her, and from that, coil
after coil unwinding, she would have entered
on the campaign of possessing her with the per-
tinacity and determination of Napoleon ad-
vancing upon Russia.

It was fortunate indeed for her that she did
not leave her room. The sight of a gay vase or a
jewelled trinket in a shop window might have
drawn her into committal of some crime.

I have said that physically she was still a

strong woman, and the weakness in her knees was more imagined than real. But she did occasionally suffer from a strange pain in the head. This was not exactly a headache; it was rather a kind of limiting of her consciousness, a constriction of the brain, as though cords were tightening over her brows and forbidding her to think. When this came upon her she was scarcely aware of what she did, moving, apparently, under the orders of some commanding personality.

It was as though some one whispered to her "Go and do this," and she then moved hypnotically. It must be repeated that she was not essentially an unkindly woman. Now that she was old and alone strange thoughts and desires possessed her. She wished ill to no one, but she moved in a world that had been largely created out of her own lingering and possessing imagination.

The picture of the fish in the green tank of water that had been her father's, that she had known ever since, as a little child, she had gazed up at it hanging in the Birmingham dining-room, had become part of her real and active world. She moved inside it as truly as she moved about the room, and the fish, especially the large one with the silver scales and the long swinging tail, left their watery confines and swam about her room slowly opening and shutting their jaws, lazily swerving in their upward or downward course.

So, too, the black-haired doll with the green dress, Miranda. Miranda had three dresses—this green one, one of ruby colour, and one of dark purple. Mrs. Payne would change the dresses from time to time and, with the change, the whole room would seem to alter. When the ruby dress was worn sunlight seemed to strike the room. The very fish were glad, and Miranda, perched up against the red candlesticks, smirked her satisfaction.

There were also the cards. With these Mrs. Payne played a game of her own, a kind of Patience maybe, but also a kind of fortune-telling, so that as she gazed at the king and queen of hearts and then lying beside them found the black, rich, thick ten of clubs, her heart beat strongly and awful destinies seemed to close about the room, and her eyes would stare far beyond those confining walls, and dynasties would rock, and the very stars would shake and quiver.

Then she would smile darkly to herself, know-

ing so much more of fate than the people about
her.

On the evening of Mrs. Amorest's visit to her
cousin she was thus playing at her cards when
the door opened and the old lady entered.   Mrs.
Amorest had had her evening meal and had felt
then an irresistible desire to talk to some one.
Endeavour to control it as she might, the promise
of her cousin that afternoon excited her so deeply
that she was shaken through and through.   One
thousand pounds a year!   To find her boy again,
to spend the little time on this earth remaining
to her with him!   To see him with her own eyes
happy!   And it was only with this sudden wonderful promise that she realised how hard things
had of late been and how, deep in her subcon-
sciousness, the fear of some tragedy, the cessation
of her money, or the running into debt and the
consequent disgrace, had played upon her.   But
now!   One thousand pounds a year!   And he
had meant it! she could still feel the touch of his
hand upon her hair.   How good he was, how
kind!   How many people had misjudged him!

She did not want to bother poor old Agatha
Payne—she always thought of her as at least
twenty years older than herself—with all her

private affairs, but she must see somebody, be kind to somebody too, because to-night she wished well to all the world.

She knocked on the door, thèn timidly stepped forward. The cards had just come out badly, meaning nothing, pretending nothing, and Agatha Payne was therefore glad to see a friend.

In a way she liked Lucy Amorest although she despised her. Poor old thing, so lonely and deserted!

She gazed up confusedly, staring through the dim light and seeing a large green fish swerve just above Mrs. Amorest's head and disappear.

"Ah, my dear! Come along!" she said.

Her voice was bass and masculine. She rose very slowly from the table, leaving the cards upon the cloth. She moved to the rocking-chair, slowly sinking down into it. A very small fire flickered in the grate. On the other side of this there was a shabby red armchair from which the stuffing burst, now here, now there, like a pale disease.

Mrs. Amorest sat down in this as on many occasions she had done before. She seemed very small and very slight beside the large fat woman, rocking, one heel in air, opposite to her.

Agatha Payne gazed at her with sombre eyes.

"You have not been out, I suppose?" said Mrs. Amorest. This was a genteel fiction always maintained between them, that to-day it was true that Mrs. Payne had not gone out, that yesterday also she had remained within, but that to-morrow, all being well, would certainly see her in the open air.

"No," said Mrs. Payne, "I have not been out. It was in no way the kind of day for me. Cold and dark. Mrs. Bloxam has kindly done my shopping for me."

"I went and paid a visit to my cousin," said Mrs. Amorest, smiling, as though she would intimate that there was far more in that visit than she could expressly say.

But Agatha Payne was a bad one for secrets. She was occupied too deeply in pursuing the strange perplexing windings of her own brain to follow closely the possibilities of another.

One thing she always did—she overlooked Mrs. Amorest and was discontented that she refused to have anywhere about her a bright spot of colour. That grey dress and plain hair and quiet little face irritated her. Poor little old thing, she would think, how old and shrivelled up she is. *She's* not long for this world!

And the sense to-night that Lucy Amorest was pleased about something—it mattered not what—irritated her still more. What right had *she* to be pleased with her poverty and mean way of dressing? So, very soon, she was in an irritable temper, muttering to herself and kicking in air her red-heeled shoe.

"And so you've begun a fire!" said Mrs. Amorest brightly. "Well, I'm sure it's time, and yet I can't make up my mind to it. I said to Mrs. Bloxam this morning that I thought to-morrow I really would start one. And yet I don't know. The winter hasn't truly come, has it? And we may get quite a number of warm days yet."

Mrs. Payne, lying back shapeless in her chair began:

"I'm sorry for you, Lucy. There's that cousin of yours, rich as he is, does nothing for you, and your boy been gone for years, no one knows where. I'm glad my child died. She would only have been a grief to me."

"He'll come back, Brand, I mean." Mrs. Amorest spoke confidently. "I feel to-night as though everything is going to turn out well. Don't you feel that way sometimes?"

"Brand? Is that your boy's name? Queer name."

"It was my husband who wished it. I think it's a nice name."

"Well, I don't think much of your Brand. Why doesn't he write and tell you what he is doing? Perhaps he's dead."

Mrs. Amorest knew well that Agatha Payne was doing her best to be provoking. She had on many occasions been through just this same conversation before, and when she had been tired, hungry, and lonely it had been difficult not to burst into tears. But she was accustomed now, and to-night she was too truly happy to care.

"I know that he's not dead," she answered. "Brand was the kind of boy who would never own that he was beaten. It was always the same, in cricket and in football. He'll tell me where he is when he's made his fortune. I'm expecting to hear any day now."

"You've been expecting to hear any day ever since I've known you," said Agatha Payne. "You're a patient woman."

Slowly, from the sluggish levels of her mind

curiosity was arising. What was making Lucy Amorest so happy to-night? What news had she received? Had some fortune come to her?

The fish swam slowly back into their deep green tank; she sat up in her chair, and with her hands on the arms and her heavy breast bulging beneath her wrapper she looked attentively at her companion.

"What's the matter with you, Lucy?" she asked. "You've had some good news."

"Well, in a way I have," Mrs. Amorest confessed. "And yet it's not news exactly. My cousin spoke to me in a very kindly way this afternoon."

"Did he say he'd leave you something in his will?" asked Mrs. Payne, her interest growing very sharply.

"He did say something," answered Mrs. Amorest, smiling a little. "Of course he may have meant nothing by it. I certainly mustn't rely on it."

"Nonsense!" said Mrs. Payne, leaning now eagerly forward. "What did he say he'd leave you?"

"Well, he *said* a thousand pounds a year!"

Mrs. Payne sank back into the chair.

"A thousand pounds! A thousand pounds a year!" Her large black eyes widened and extended. "Why, Lucy, that's a fortune!"

"Yes," said Mrs. Amorest faintly, "it is. And that's why I don't want to rely on it. It's only what he *said*, of course."

"And was there any one else there when he said it?"

"No, there wasn't. We were quite alone, and he was very kind indeed. I have never known him so nice."

Agatha Payne stared. A thousand pounds a year! And to be given to that poor little mouse who had only a few years to live at the best. What would *she* do with a thousand pounds a year? whereas the things that Agatha Payne might do . . . the gay, glorious, coloured, glittering things that she might buy! And there suddenly came into her head the idea that she herself would have some of this money that was coming to Lucy Amorest. She was a weak, good-natured, little creature was Lucy Amorest. She would give anything away. She would do anything for anybody.

Her heart beat. It was strange, perhaps, that with her passion for gay things she had not, long ago, spent more than she had and encumbered herself with debt. But an odd laziness held her captive, and perhaps also the old house had thrown some spell over her. It had forbidden her perhaps to leave it. (Old houses can do such things. They can impregnate human souls with their own subtle poison and with bricks and beams of wood and flakes of mortar wall in the human body as surely as in the cruel past errant wives and sinning nuns were confined.

Here was something beneath her hand. She smiled, and a grim forbidding smile it was.

"That's right, Lucy. Don't you count on it. You come to me and we'll talk it over. There's nothing like a little plan. Nothing."

Mrs. Amorest was frightened. She did not know why. It had been foolish of her to say anything at all about the money. It had been, in a way, betraying the confidence of her cousin.

She was tired, and needed the security of her own room.

"I think I'll go to bed now," she said. "It's late."

Mrs. Payne smiled once more. "You come in again and we'll talk it over," she said.

Mrs. Amorest said good-night and went.

She hurried into her room, lit her lamp, and began to undress. She took the photograph of her boy from the mantelpiece and kissed it. Then she knelt down and said her prayers.

CHAPTER III

MISS MAY BERINGER was poorer than either Mrs. Amorest or Mrs. Payne. She was not only very poor, but she had to confront the possibility of having, in some six months or so, no money whatever. Literally no money. Nothing.

She was as absolutely alone in the world as it was possible for any one to be—at least she would have been so had it not been for her dog Pip.

People talk of poverty and they talk of loneliness, and in a majority of cases do not understand the true meaning of either word. People also talk of "the working classes" and their hardships. Very seldom do you hear anything about the "poor gentlewoman classses" and *their* hardships. The poor gentlewomen of this world do, in every civilised country, by their unselfish and heroic lives, constitute a large proportion of the

future citizens of the Kingdom of Heaven.
Verily, they need that Paradisal promise.

Miss Beringer was one of those unfortunate
women who have never been wanted by anybody. Neither her father nor mother, none of
her numerous brothers and sisters, no relation near
or distant—none of these wanted her.

She was the daughter of a doctor of Exeter
City. She had been always, with her heavy
hooked nose, faint eyebrows, pale pasty com-
plexion and long lanky body, very homely. Nor
were the defects of her person excused by the bril-
liance of her accomplishments. She was born
and bred into a period when the daughters of
Great Britain were expected neither to spin nor
to sew but only to wait, in patient eagerness, for
the day when a gentleman would ask them in
marriage.

It was obvious from the very first that it was
unlikely that any one would beg for May's hand,
because she was plain and awkward and also
because she had three sisters older than herself.
Her unfortunate father and mother killed themselves in the attempt to win that unceasing battle
that great progeny and small incomes force upon
so many virtuous and upright citizens. Two of

May's sisters married, one died, two brothers went to the Colonies, one was killed in China and one vanished into the depths of America. May, at the age of forty, found herself with an income of one hundred and fifty pounds a year, alone in the world. That was thirty years ago—thirty years of being wanted by nobody, thirty years of finding that ends were never quite meeting, thirty years of absurdities, hopes, enthusiasms, disappointments, confusions. Confusions most of all.

May Beringer was unfortunately a stupid woman. A stupid woman with a kind and generous heart, than that there is nothing more aggravating, exasperating, touching, and pathetic to be found in the human kingdom. Her stupidity was not altogether her own fault. In the first place she had never had any education. Her mother and father had not wished that "their girls" should go to a rough day-school where they would assuredly learn rude habits from rough day-girls. A governess had therefore been supplied, and because finances were so low only the poorest kind of governess could be afforded, and because the family was so large even the finest kind of governess would have been unable to deal with the situation adequately. May Beringer, therefore, had learnt nothing save that Oliver Cromwell executed Charles I. and that the Amazon was a river in America, and of these two facts she was not very certain. Moreover, she was quite unaware that she was ill-educated. Facts in the days when she was a girl were divided into divisions of the Improper, the Masculine, and the Unnecessary. With the first of these she must, of course, have nothing to do, the second she left to the men, the third were waste of time. She was therefore never challenged as to her ignorance. She was not in the least a modern girl of her time. She read only the idlest fictions, played all games very badly, and when she found that her ideas refused to clarify sufficiently for coherent conversation, took refuge in giggling silence.

Beneath all this her heart was warm, eager, and sentimental. She longed to be good and kind and generous. She did not care whether people liked her or no, all that she wished was to be allowed to like them. She adored her father and mother, loved her brothers and sisters indiscriminately, and felt romantic passions for every man who came to their house. She did not expect a proposal of marriage. She had been told very often by her frank and careless brothers and sisters that she was plain, awkward, and stupid. She had from the very earliest age developed a terror of almost everything and everybody. Her very shyness and gaucherie made her timid and then as she was conscious of her mistakes her shyness increased.

She felt that she might be very brilliant and amusing could she only arrange her ideas in order, but always something unfortunate came in the way—she sat down when she ought to stand up, spoke when she should be silent, smiled when she should have frowned.

Then her body was clumsy, untidy. Do what she would her clothes were for ever in disorder.

She lived alone in Exeter from the years of forty to sixty. She occupied the upper part of a little house near the Cathedral and it was there that she spent the happiest part of her life. She managed on her tiny income because her father's solicitor saw that she received it in moderation, a little at a time; he paid her rent; he also let it be understood in the principal shops of the town that she was not to be permitted to run up accounts. She had at first a gay and fanciful fashion of going into a shop, looking around her happily, and then saying, "Oh, I'll have that! Would you kindly send it this afternoon?" The shopmen kindly agreed, but it was not sent, and by the following day she had quite forgotten that she had ever ordered it.

She was happy during this time in her two rooms, in her few friends, and, latterly, in the friend whom she adored, Jane Betts. It was essential to her nature that she should adore some one, and if there was no one positively close at hand then she would choose some one out of the illustrated papers or one of the Royal Family.

Jane Betts was younger than she, daughter of a retired Colonel, a bright jolly woman of thirty or so, to whom life was a joke and everything a cause for wonder. She accepted the affection of May Beringer with amused acquiescence, and then suddenly, on a day, perceived something touching and even beautiful in this plain elderly woman's devotion. Where another would have been wearied or bored Jane was moved and grateful. Something serious entered into her life that had never been there before.

There followed for May Beringer the six glorious months of her life, the only truly happy

time that she was ever to know. It is for ever
marvellous what happy love can do for the divine
soul and the awkward human body. Had fate
willed it and the friendship lasted, May Beringer
might have known transformation. Already,
guided by the gentle hints of her friend, awkward-
ness was leaving her, comeliness was approaching
her, a novel orderliness was mastering her poor
confused brains, happiness shone from her eyes,
people were beginning to say that "she wasn't
so bad after all."

It was during the Christmas of that happy six
months that Jane gave her friend that piece of
red amber that was afterwards to play so
important a part in May's life. It became, of
course, her most cherished possession.

Then, alas, a large red-faced Colonel arrived
from India on leave, saw Jane, fell instantly in
love with her in spite of her thirty years, pro-
posed and was accepted. That was a terrible day
when Jane told her friend of what had occurred,
and May Beringer showed in the fashion with
which she received the news the stuff of which she
was beginning to be made. She said that all that
she wished was that Jane should be happy: she
was sorry indeed that Jane was going so far, but

that, of course, neither seas nor the passing of the years should ever divide them. Unfortunately, seas and long absences are more powerful separators than friends and lovers in the full flood of their romantic ideals will honestly realise. Moreover the red-faced Colonel did not appreciate his darling Jane's friend. It was the one thing in his darling Jane that he could not understand, that she should care for that "old giggling scarecrow." And then, unfortunately, May perceived that he did not like her, and forgetting her hard-won control only a few nights before Jane's departure lost her temper and called the Colonel names. After that followed floods of tears, urgent agonising demands for forgiveness, touching reconciliations. But it may be that Jane left Exeter feeling that her good old May might in the passing of the years have become something of a good old nuisance.

It was after Jane's departure that May Beringer "took to dogs." She suddenly discovered, as many other human beings have discovered both before and since, that dogs are marvellously unaware of faults and deficiencies only too obvious to all one's friends and acquaintances, that they bear one no grudges, that when you have lost your temper and behaved abominably they take your sins upon them and ask for your forgiveness, that they have no irony nor cynicism, that they are not pessimistic, and the sight of a bone or a cat or a pat on the head is enough to make them believe that all is well with the world, and that do you but treat them kindly they will prefer you to all other human beings whatever and will exhibit that same preference in a most flattering and self-justifying manner.

To a woman of May Beringer's sentiment a dog was the perfect solution. She was not, however, by nature adapted to look after dogs successfully. For some years dogs inevitably died under her hand, and she passed through a series of soul-searching griefs swearing that she would never have another, that Gyp or Tray or Fido was surely the very last. But dog succeeded dog, and apartment succeeded apartment, landladies invariably liking the Fido or the Gyp of the moment less than did their adoring mistress.

Then, finding Exeter difficult, expensive, and the perpetual echo of Jane's dear voice, she moved into the country. She went to St. Lennan, a small seaside resort on the coast of North

Glebeshire. At first it seemed that here she had met good fortune. She was now sixty years of age but was strong and healthy. She took two rooms on the sea-front from a kindly widow who had no objections at all to dogs and indeed preferred them. The winter months in North Glebeshire are bleak and wild indeed, but May Beringer threw herself into the clerical work of the parish with eager enthusiasm. She adored the clergyman and slaved for him. The clergyman was at first grateful, but soon it became apparent that Miss Beringer was a breeder of disputes and a begetter of quarrels. She wanted things her own way, and, in spite of her timidity, was touchy and sensitive to a fault. Moreover, she could not be relied on to carry anything forward to completeness. Her eagerness was not balanced by forethought nor her devotion by clear thinking.

So, after a year or two, May Beringer found herself isolated once more, and abandoned to the company of a few old maids like herself, her landlady, and her dog. She did not complain. She was always only too ready to admit that everything was her own fault.

She had acquired a passion for St. Lennan.

There was something about its wind-swept sandy shore, about the fashion in which the hard green breakers split suddenly into jade and foam, slipping down into silky splendour, something in the naked line of houses, the low bare hill, the circling arm of the dim white shore that won her heart. It was cold, it was chill, but it was her own.

In the summer it was not hers. Never at any time a popular resort, there were nevertheless during the summer months families sufficient for her to feel that she was old and ugly and unwanted. Then the dog of the moment was always in trouble at that time, lured by little girls, tempted by little boys, above all excited and bemused by the presence of other dogs.

Every morning about mid-day, weather foul or fair, May Beringer might be seen robed in a long green jacket and wearing a large hard hat stuck through with a large sharp pin, striding along the shore, a small dog tethered to her with a chain. She liked small dogs, but not too small, and fox terriers were her favourites. She had, ere this, by sheer force of necessity learnt something of their proper care. They were not, as a rule, very healthy animals, and wore a strange air of bewilderment, fostered, one may imagine, by the puzzling moods to which their mistress was subject, slapping them one moment and hugging them the next.

It was when she was sixty-five and had been at St. Lennan some five years that she received the dog, Pip. She received him as a puppy from the landlady, who felt that she had not been, in the past, altogether kind to the queer and lonely old woman. Pip seemed from the beginning to understand better than any of his predecessors the purposes for which he was born into this world. He was not a handsome dog, and one coal-black ear, the rest of his body being white, gave him rather a ludicrous appearance. Nor was he intelligent. His mind was, strangely like his mistress's, compact of fear and confusion. They say that animals resemble very frequently their masters, or, maybe, masters their animals. There was, as Pip developed into maturer years, a quite ludicrous resemblance to his mistress. His body was lanky and ill-controlled like hers, his mind, as I have said, confused and panic-stricken, and he had exactly the same loving and eager heart. He was more fortunate than his mistress in this, that there was no question as to the true altar of his devotion. He loved one and one alone, he

saw in her no absurdities, no oddities, no stupid-
ities. It is true that he must often have been
puzzled by her moods, but just as Mrs. Amorest
was always assured that God's actions, whatever
they might be, were for the best, so felt Pip
about his mistress.

He was, during the years at St. Lennan, a
happy dog. Except for those few weeks in the
summer he might run riotously along that un-
ending beach pursuing imaginary cats, sticks, and
bones, barking at the breakers as they rolled
towards him, confident in his own fine security,
returning to those warm rooms where his beloved
mistress awaited him, where there was food and
warmth and unfailing affection.

In her sixty-eighth year May Beringer met
upon the sands a wise old gentleman with silvery
hair and a benevolent cape who talked with her
in the kindest fashion. They spoke together day
after day. He was, it appeared, a professor of
Oxford University. He liked her very much and
discovered her to be most intelligent and far-
seeing. It was the month of June and the days
were warm.

She told him everything of her life, speaking
even to him of her beloved Jane. He became,

after a short interval, so warm a friend that he begged to know whether her money were properly invested. The old solicitor friend of her family was dead. The son, who had succeeded to his father's position, took in the old lady less personal an interest, and it was not long 'before the kind old professor with the silvery hair had invested her money so carefully for her that she was never to see any of it again. Most of it— luckily not all. There remained to her some hundred and fifty pounds.

The shock to her when she discovered what had occurred added to the confusion of her already confused brain. She could not understand how so charming an old man could have done anything so cruel. She wrote to him again and again, but, of course, received no reply. The thing that hurt her the most was not the loss of her money, but that she had confided to him so many intimacies about her friendship with dear Jane.

She cried about that in the dark silences of the over-long night.

Something had to be done. She collected what remained of her fortune and had the confused idea of going to Polchester and finding there some

work. What work? Governess, perhaps. It was
true that she was now seventy, but she was strong
and active. At least in St. Lennan there was no
work to be found. Her heart failed her did she
positively visualise to herself what work, any
work at her age, would mean, so she did not
visualise it; she simply ordered her few pieces of
furniture to be packed and sent to a Polchester
depository, said farewell to her kind landlady,
and departed, Pip chained to her side.

Arrived in Polchester she stayed for a while
in rooms at the top of Orange Street, but these
were expensive; she had her own bits of furniture; where was the cheapest place?

The cheapest place was Pontippy Square.

The first vision of the bare room at the top of
that old tumbling house frightened her, but the
rent was so small that she felt that it would be
wicked to refuse it. She would be here, too, her
own mistress—no one could interfere with her.
She was told that two other ladies were tenants
on this same floor. She would have company if
she wished. Real ladies like herself.

Only she said nothing about dogs. Were dogs
allowed? She did not enquire. Here surely no
one would interfere with her, but on the whole

it was safer not to enquire. So she settled in. The depository sent up her possessions—her old dark blue carpet with the large ink spot in one corner and showing the threads in another corner where a youthful Pip had gnawed it, her bed, her round mahogany table, her four mahogany chairs, her two dark blue armchairs, her bookcase, her two oil paintings "after Cuyp," and her chest of drawers. She had also her photographs of her father, her mother, a family group, Jane Betts, and Pip. She had her two Venetian vases —*and* her piece of red amber.

This was a very fine piece. It stood in the middle of the mantelpiece, shining and gleaming. Jane Betts had seen it, that famous Christmas, in the shop windows of an Exeter antiquarian and, feeling very tender towards her "dear silly old May," had gone in and bought it. "It will warm you, my dear," she said when she gave it to her, "always keep you warm like my affection. Never lose it or sell it. My heart is inside it!"

You know how sentimental people can be! Jane Betts was, in her nature, something of a cynic, and her marriage with the red-faced Colonel made her in after life yet more cynical, but those months of friendship with May Beringer touched, for a moment, her truest, sincerest affection. She did not know it, but she was never again to care for any one so deeply as she did for that ugly, awkward, lanky old woman.

So did this chunk of amber enshrine both their affections. It was shaped square like a little block of wood, and this block was surmounted with a carved red amber dragon. It had in it the most lovely lights and colours, that flashed and trembled from the deepest Venetian red to the fairest honey gold.

When the shimmer of the fire or the light of the lamp caught it, it did indeed seem to be stirring with the fire of its own heart. The dragon raised its head, his eyes shot flame.

For May Beringer it was simply the heart of her life. There, enshrined in that lovely thing, was all the happiness of her days. So long as that remained to her she could not, as dear Jane had said, be altogether cold and chill.

Pip settled into the new room very easily. He had his cushion in the corner near the fire; he gave his mistress one look to see whether she really intended that it was here that they were going to live, and then when he saw that that was so, behaved as though he had never known any other home.

May Beringer knew not a single soul in Polchester. Never before in her life had she been in a place where she knew nobody. She missed the kind landlady of St. Lennan very badly, but guarded herself against talking to strangers, being warned by her experience with the silver-haired gentleman.

But she liked the town greatly. It reminded her of Exeter, and yet there were not associations with dear Jane at every step. She was soon a familiar figure up and down the High Street and at the Cathedral services. She was remarkably straight-backed and tall for her years, and people called her "the old Grenadier."

There was something comic about her, with her sallow face, her hooked nose, her old-fashioned garments, and the fox terrier trotting at her side. People always noticed her and wondered who she was. A little cracked, they thought she must be.

"Grenadier" was in fact the very last thing to call her. I said in my first account of her that she had always been frightened of everything; now, with her old age, her fears had accumulated upon her. Alone in this strange town, with no friend in the world, it was natural enough that she should know fear. There is a fear that comes upon lonely old people that is like no other fear. It is a fear bred of loneliness —the sight and sound of all these hurrying multitudes pressing in upon you, hurrying past you, looking with hard, careless eyes into yours. You are near the end of your days, you have lived all your life upon the earth, and this is what it has come to, that there is not a living soul who needs you nor thinks of you. Death is approaching, and there will be no one to be with you at the last. It were surely better that you had never been born.

In May Beringer's case there was this to be added, that soon—in six months' time or so— she would have no money. Unless she obtained some work what would happen to her? Work! As she looked at the crowds that passed her in the High Street and the Market-place she did not know how she would ever begin to ask for work. Had she been a peasant there would be things that she would have learnt to do. Like Mrs. Bloxam, she might have gone out charing.

But because she was born a lady she could do nothing. Nothing.

Mrs. Bloxam was her one comfort. That kindly woman, after the first day or two and her natural reaction against a "messy dog"—when she had observed too that Pip, the animal, was not a bad dog at all, very clean in his habits and devoted to his mistress—decided that the poor old maid needed her services quite as badly as did the other two old women—more, indeed, because Mrs. Amorest had a quiet, assured courage of her own, and Mrs. Payne, although she was "that queer you never would believe unless you saw her," nevertheless had her own private sources of satisfaction. No, "that poor old Miss Beringer" needed her the most.

Mrs. Bloxam spent more than her fair share of time in that house, as her husband was for ever telling her. She had plenty of other work to be busy over, and more paying work too, but her "old ladies" were her chiefest charge. "Poor old sillies," she called them—"living all alone top of that shaking old house—shouldn't like——" she half-apologised to her husband. He when sober admired her and when drunk abused her, whatever she did, so that his opinion was of no very great value.

But her furrowed crimson face, her large round features, her charwoman straw hat stuck askew on one side of her head, her queer hoarse laugh as though she had a tankard of ale in front of her mouth, her way of standing, her thick legs spread, her head back, her hands on her ample hips—all these things were soon jewels beyond price to May Beringer, who, in no time at all, was telling her everything about her life even to the intimacies of her friendship with dear Jane.

At this point she always cried a little, and even Mrs. Bloxam rubbed one eye with the back of her hand, that was of the texture of alligator skin.

"To see that poor old dear sitting up in bed with her grey hair all about her face, with her old green muffler round her throat—poor worm! —you can't but pity her."

"You'm too soft-'earted—that's what's the matter with you, Jennifer," said Mr. Bloxam, sober for the moment. But Mrs. Bloxam was no angel, and to see her in one of her tempers was to be reminded of the Homeric ages. But May Beringer saw her at her best—for the time being, at any rate.

CHAPTER IV

RED AMBER

IT was not until the second Sunday after her arrival in Pontippy Square that May Beringer met Mrs. Amorest and Mrs. Payne.

It was a cold Sunday morning. From her bed May Beringer could see the sun like a red orange above the grey roofs of the houses. The houses were threaded with white frost, the smoke rose against the grey sky a greyer shadow, and the limbs of the one tree were silver-lined.

Did she move her head the sun appeared also to move and to rock in friendly greeting, and because the glass of the window was rough and coarse-grained the sun swelled as though with sudden ribaldry and then ran thin and tight like a drawn string.

It was warm in bed and cosy and faintly the bells could be heard. Two sparrows came hopping to the window and then a robin. Very soon her breakfast would come in and she could give

them something. She had told Mrs. Bloxam
that she would always have a boiled egg on Sunday as an extra to the toast and potted meat that
was her customary fare.

At the thought of the egg she smiled and sat
up in bed, bending over to the chair for her
green sweater; she tied the arms of this tightly
round her neck, allowing the body of it to fall
over her breast, then she looked for the piece of
amber and saw that it was there secure although
scarcely visible in the dim light. Then she
looked through the window again and saw the
faintest thread of pale blue break the grey. So
it would be a fine day. A fine clear frosty
Sunday! Could anything be nicer?

A moment later Pip was at the door welcoming Mrs. Bloxam, who arrived carrying pressed
against her mountainous bosom a tray, and her
black bonnet with black bugles (her Sunday
wear) was pushed to the back of her head and
her face was all smiles.

"Now, here's a nice Sunday sirprise, my
dear," she shouted (she always shouted at her
old ladies although they were none of them
deaf). "There's that kind woman giving you
one of her sausages this morning."

"What woman?" asked Miss Beringer.

"Why, to be sure, Mrs. Hamorest of course. I'd 'ardly been in 'er room two minutes when she says, 'Mrs. Bloxam,' she says, 'there's a sausage more than I can manage,' she says. 'I've been wondering whether Miss Bellringer' (Mrs. Bloxam's perversions were always of kindly intention) 'would like one,' she says. 'Of course, I 'aven't exactly called on 'er, but we're all friends in this 'ouse,' she says, 'or I'm sure we ought to be. You just ask 'er, Mrs. Bloxam. I know Mrs. Payne don't care for sausages,' she says; 'it's just waste giving them to 'er.' 'Why, mum,' I says to 'er, 'Miss Bellringer looks just the sort of lady to relish a sausage, and it's a friendly feeling in you, mum,' I says, 'and if Sunday isn't a day to be friendly on, where *will* we all be?' I says. Poor worm! and 'er looking so pretty sitting up in bed with 'er kind thoughts and 'er snow-white 'air and 'er pretty little ways. So I just brought it along, miss, feelin' sure you'd relish it, and I've cooked it to a turn in Mrs. Hamorest's frying-pan—you just wait, my pretty, your turn's coming. Almost 'uman, miss, isn't 'e? More 'uman than some, I'm thinking."

During this time Mrs. Bloxam was arranging

Miss Beringer's bed, patting and pushing the pillows, smoothing the sheets, and setting the tray so that it sat evenly over Miss Beringer's lap. When that lady saw the tea, the egg, the buttered toast, the crisp and bursting sausage, her pale face flushed. Not a bad beginning to a pleasant Sunday. And she must go in and thank Mrs. Amorest. She was longing for a friend. She ached to love somebody again. Mrs. Bloxam entertained her with gossip, giving her detailed horrors out of the *Sunday News* with infinite relish and gusto, lit the fire, tidied the room, took away the tray again, and departed.

Then May Beringer sank back into slumber again, the easy slumber of the old, and lying there, the green muffler yet tied about her neck, so pale she was and still that it might have been death that held her.

The clock ticked on, the dog also slept, there was not a sound in the house. Then when it was nearly two o'clock, a coal fell out of the dying fire and crashed upon the grate, Pip woke and barked, up Miss Beringer started thinking the house on fire. She looked at the clock, and seeing how late it was, was soon out of bed. She washed in water icy cold, put on the warmest under-clothing she had, and that was not warm enough. But she had been given by the landlady at St. Lennan a grey knitted woollen waistcoat, and this was a great comfort to her now. Her best clothes were her dark red jacket and skirt. The skirt was short both for the period and her age, but they were not yet faded and they were warm. She stared at herself in the little looking-glass over the wash-hand stand and was pleased. She looked young for her age, she thought. She was strong and healthy. It was not so absurd that she should find work as governess and companion.

For a moment her fears left her. She was brave and optimistic and happy. Full of this spirit she went out, Pip closely at her heel, crossed the passage, and knocked on Mrs. Amorest's door.

"Come in," said a little faint voice, and, entering, she was at once charmed—charmed with the neatness and tidiness of the room, some red-brown chrysanthemums in a thin silver vase, the old rose-coloured chairs, the blue and silver scene beyond the window, the orange fire faint like paper beneath the winter sun that flooded the place, and then the little woman with her snow-white hair, her beautiful hands, and the smile that shone in her eyes as, turning, she saw her visitor.

"It must be Miss Beringer," she said, coming forward.

"Yes, it is," said May Beringer, her long body trembling with interest and excitement. "I had to come in and just thank you for being so generous, as I am sure indeed you have been, to a perfect stranger and one whom you've never seen in your life before and have no reason at all to be kind to."

Miss Beringer always said everything twice or three times. It seemed to make her statement more definite.

"You *will* sit down, won't you?" Mrs. Amorest asked, drawing one of the armchairs near to the fire. "Because we are such very near neighbours we must know one another a little."

"I'm sure that's very kind of you," said May Beringer breathlessly. "I sound as though I'd been running up a whole flight of stairs, don't I? but I haven't really. It's only my nervousness. I'm always shy at meeting any one for the first time. I've always been so ever since a child, and indeed I can't remember a time when I wasn't nervous. As quite a little girl I was as shy as anything."

"You mustn't be shy with me," said Mrs. Amorest gently. "I'm a very unalarming person. What a delightful dog!"

"Yes, isn't he? I've always been partial to dogs. I've had dogs as companions for years and years. In fact, I'm never without a dog. His name's Pip!"

"Pip! What a nice name! Come here, Pip! Come and make friends."

Pip came, seeing that his mistress wished him to do so, but no one was very real to him save his mistress. However, he licked Mrs. Amorest's hand and then lay down, his head on his paws, waiting until his mistress should wish to move.

The two ladies considered one another. While talking amiably they were taking in one another's points. Each was thinking the other really old and pitying a little, but each needed a friend.

It was nevertheless very soon evident that May Beringer would be clay in the hands of Mrs. Amorest, and when that old lady realised that it was so there came into her heart not contempt (she felt contempt for no human being) but a little sigh, perhaps of regret. What she wanted was some one stronger than herself, some one on whose opinion she could rely, some one who would give her true and wise advice. It was very soon evident that May Beringer would be no projector of wise advice!

They talked a little, keeping their own confidences, and soon a silence fell. It was then that Mrs. Amorest said, "Now, I wonder. I had been thinking of going to the Cathedral service this afternoon. Would you care to come too?"

As soon as she said it she wished that she had not, for reasons that were, for her, weak and snobbish. Poor Miss Beringer would attract attention walking into the Cathedral: her face was odd, her clothes were odd, and Mrs. Amorest was sure that her walk would be odd. Mrs. Amorest, absolutely courageous though she was, hated to attract attention by any eccentricity. She hoped that Miss Beringer would decline, but at once, when she saw the light in Miss Beringer's eyes and heard the happiness in her voice as she said, "Thank you. I'll most certainly come. I'll go with you with pleasure," she was glad that she had suggested it. She thought to herself, "Poor old thing, she must be terribly lonely," and at that very same moment May Beringer was thinking to *herself*, "Poor old thing, I'm sure she's as lonely as anything. It must be wonderful to have some one to go with."

So they went very happily together, slowly down the stairs because the stairs were dark although it was early afternoon, and then slowly through the streets because it was a cold and frosty afternoon. That at any rate was the reason that they gave to one another. The real reason was that their limbs were not so strong nor so active as they had been.

They still did not give one another any confidences, May Beringer having in her mind always the old man with the silvery hair, and Mrs. Amorest because, in spite of her recent rashness with Agatha Payne, she was very good at keeping her own counsel.

Nevertheless, by the time that they had reached the high Cathedral door they were very good friends: May Beringer because she wanted some one to love willy-nilly, and Mrs. Amorest because she was touched by May Beringer's apparent helplessness. Within the quiet of the Cathedral they were happy indeed. They sat in the back of the nave unnoticed by anybody, and although the seats might have been more comfortable (and why, indeed, are they not more comfortable?) they were very glad to sit down and rest.

Mrs. Amorest knew the Cathedral by heart. She liked always to have the same place in the nave, almost the place where she was now sitting; thence she could see to her right framed between two pillars the window that had the pictures of the boy Christ, Christ with His mother, Christ playing with the boys by the river-side, Christ in the workshop, and the others.

She loved the colours, mistily purple and green and olive, but she loved it also for its subject, thinking of her own son, as she loved to do, when he had been small and helpless and divinely in need of her. Those days seemed to her but of yesterday, and closing her eyes she could see the bright blue Glebeshire skies and the sharp jagged teeth of the rocks, the valley running to the very lap of the sand, the white cottage set like a determined foot on the brow of the patient hill. Ambrose working at his poetry in the upstairs room with the slanting roof, and Brand in the garden crawling across the tiny plot of green to pull the cat's tail. . . .

All that she would see, and much more, as the organ wandered from pillar to pillar as though it were searching for her, and suddenly the clergyman's voice rose cutting the dimness and calling her to her prayers. She was never so near to her son as in that church, and while she stayed, her eyes closed, a hand seemed ,to be laid upon her brow and a voice to whisper to her that all was well with her, and that she must be at peace.

She did not fear; she feared nor man nor woman nor life nor death—only God. But to-day instinctively as she sat there she realised that the woman next to her was compact of fear. She did not know how she had realised it, but this was true, and once again, as in her room, a little tremor of irritation shook her. She did not care for helpless people. Never in her life had she done so. She admired nothing so much as independence and courage, and perhaps that was the one lesson that life still had to teach her—tenderness for the weak. There was nothing she had admired so much in her son as his independence. She admired it also in old Agatha Payne.

But here was a woman who would, she foresaw, in no time at all, be depending upon her, wanting her advice, her assistance, her authority.

Poor old thing! Mrs. Amorest, as they rose together to listen to the anthem, felt kindly indeed, and, because the anthem was Wesley's "Wilderness," her whole maternal being rose up in poor Miss Beringer's service. So much can familiar music do!

Miss Beringer, for her part, was not thinking overmuch of her companion. She was thinking of the comfort that it was to sit down, but the seats were hard, and there was a nice cosy light over everything—pretty place—pretty place— sleepy, sleepy—strangely sleepy . . . and then jerked awake to hear, far far away, the reading of the First Lesson.

No, she did not consider Mrs. Amorest very deeply, save that she wanted to love her. She wanted to love somebody, quickly, immediately, somebody of her own class with whom she could go for walks, and somebody, too, whom one could depend upon, somebody who would find work for her and advise her, and also somebody who would allow her to have her own way when she wanted it.

This old lady seemed really what she needed —old, of course, poor old dear, but then that

was so pleasant for Miss Beringer to be of use
to some one who needed her.

"The Wilderness and the Solitary Place . . ."
sang the choir. At once May Beringer saw the
long white stretch of the St. Lennan sands, the
gulls wheeling with discordant cries through the
grey air:

> The Wilderness and the Solitary Place
> Shall be glad—glad—glad—

Her legs were aching. Just below the knee there
was a strange grinding pain. She looked about
her to see whether any one were sitting down.
No one immediately close to her, and Mrs.
Amorest as straight as a stick, her little head up
like a bird's—a stick and a bird! A stick and
a bird!

"The Wilderness and the Solitary Place."
Truly the pain that had crept up now into her
knees was too bad to be borne. She sat down.
Mrs. Amorest did not turn her head, but May
Beringer would like to have whispered, "It is
not because I am truly tired, but I have to-day
a pain in my knee. I can stand as well as you,
but to-day I have a pain. Any one might
have it."

And then she fell asleep, quite suddenly, and dreamt of Jane Betts. The general murmur of prayer which seemed to her in her dream to be the rustle of mice in the straw—she was about to call out to Jane "Take care, dear! Look out for the mice!"—aroused her. She slipped down upon her knees. They hurt her badly, and the wooden prayer-stool cut into her very bone. She could not think of her prayers because of the pain, but vaguely behind the pain ran the mice scampering about in her head. Afraid of what? Of the cat perhaps. A large dark cat with green eyes. She shuddered, and fear came down upon her like a large grasping hand, and she was glad that she could feel Mrs. Amorest's shoulder against her.

They walked home through the velvet-frosted dark. The dark, studded with stars and lights on the hills like the eyes of innumerable animals watching. Not cats, because they were not green, but tigers and lions, lions and tigers.

She explained this to Mrs. Amorest. They were walking very slowly because they were both extremely tired, but they would not mention this.

"They are like the eyes of lions and tigers," May Beringer said.

But Mrs. Amorest was thinking of the money that her cousin was going to leave her, and she did not hear. One thousand pounds! One thousand pounds! What might she not do? She and Brand together. . . .

"Yes," she said, "don't they sing beautifully? Especially that boy. . . . There's something about a boy's voice that always makes me want to cry. Silly, of course. . . ."

Poor old thing! She was deaf then as well as old! Poor old thing! When May Beringer spoke next she shouted, but still Mrs. Amorest's mind was distant, and they arrived in Pontippy Square in silence, two very very weary old women.

Slowly, slowly they mounted the stairs, stopping on every landing for breath; and it was as though when they stood there they were listening for some one or something. They could hear only the beating of their hearts.

Arrived on their own floor May Beringer, breathless, gasped, "I always make a cup of tea about this time. I wonder whether you would come and drink it with me?"

Mrs. Amorest said that she would be delighted. "A minute to take my hat off."

When, later, she came into May Beringer's room she exclaimed with pleasure, "What nice things you have!" May Beringer's heart went out, bursting with love, to the dear old thing looking so charming there in the middle of the floor, with her neat little figure, her beautiful hair, her sparkling eyes. Here *was* some one to love indeed!

Mrs. Amorest admired everything,—the blue carpet, the round mahogany table, the four mahogany chairs, the arm-chairs, the bookcase, the pictures after Cuyp,—especially the bookcase.

"I do love reading, don't you, Miss Beringer? What have you got here? Mrs. Henry Wood! She writes *good* stories, I think. And those volumes of *Good Words*. I shall ask you to lend me one some day. And Sir Walter Scott. My husband always used to say that Sir Walter Scott had the true romantic spirit, although a little old-fashioned of course. But then my husband was more modern than I was. As of course he would be, being a writer. He wrote plays and poetry, and was very well known in his time.

Very well known indeed. Ah! I see you have Tennyson. Don't you love 'The Idylls of the King'? I do. That one about Guinevere is such a beautiful tale, I think, but sad, of course. Terribly sad. But then they did wrong, poor things, and it was right that they should be punished. Still, I can never help but be sorry for them a little. Tennyson was such a *noble* poet, I think. Perhaps a little *too* noble sometimes. Don't you think people can be *too* noble, Miss Beringer, just now and again?"

Mrs. Amorest's eyes twinkled as she straightened herself after looking at the bookcase. That was what her husband used to call "her wicked, sarcastic side"—the side of her that he had never understood, so that she had been forced to drive it under during their married life, but even now, after all these years, it would on occasion break out.

She moved around admiring everything, while May Beringer saw to the kettle. She saw then the piece of red amber. She stopped where she was, lost in wonder.

"Oh dear! What a beautiful thing!"

"Yes," said May Beringer, her voice awed and

reverent, "that was given me by my dearest friend."

"How wonderful! I really never have seen anything so beautiful. May I pick it up for a moment?"

"Certainly. Do look at it." May Beringer's voice shook with pride.

When Mrs. Amorest had it in her hand she was pleased indeed. She loved beautiful things, but beautiful things were always so remote, behind shop windows, in museums or picture-galleries, always ticketed and catalogued and, above your head, a notice that said "Don't touch."

When her hands closed about this and she felt its coldness and its strength, when she held it up to the light and saw the shaft of gold strike through to its very heart, when she saw the liquid bubbles of rich ruby red that danced in the cleft of thick, honey-coloured, misted fibre, when she saw the dragon with his flaming head and gold-flashing claws, when she felt its sturdiness and independence and form, she could only say and exclaim, as she replaced it reverently on the mantelpiece:

"You *are* fortunate to have it! It lights up all the room."

May Beringer *was* pleased! To praise her red amber was to praise her Jane Betts, and to bring straight back there into the room all that warm friendship and love, all those happy days. The kettle was boiling. The biscuits were spread upon the blue plate, the bread and butter was cut. They sat down happily to the round mahogany table.

"I have had a strange pain in my knee to-day," said May Beringer. "I think it must be the frost. I wonder whether the frost can have given me a pain in my knee. I really never have anything the matter with me. As a rule there's nothing the matter with me at all."

"Well," said Mrs. Amorest, "I don't wonder. This sudden cold weather can give any one anything. Now have you any Elliman's? Because I've always found that rubbing in a little Elliman's last thing at night is quite wonderful. Now if you haven't any I'd be only too glad——"

There was a knock on the door. Both ladies were startled. "Come in," said Miss Beringer.

The door slowly opened, then there was an interval during which nothing happened save that Pip drew back towards his mistress, growl-

ing. Then Mrs. Payne came forward. To Miss
Beringer, unprepared for her, she must have been
amazing enough. She was wearing her old red
wrapper and her .crimson shoes. Through her
hair was stuck the black comb with the glass
diamonds. Her shapeless body, her large heavy
bosom, her high colour—one of the raggle-taggle
gipsies indeed, hemispheres apart from the two
Englishwomen who sat there looking at her.

She had been going to speak, her mouth had
opened, a smile had been preparing, but at the
instant of entering she had been transfixed, even
as Lot's wife on looking back to the accursed
cities of the Plains. She stared, her eyes, large
and black and piercing, were held as though by
the glory of the Lord; she put her hand up to
her breast and, breathing deeply, seeing neither
of the women in front of her nor anything in the
room save the mantelpiece and its contents, gazed.

It had been unusual enough for her to leave
her room. The cause had been the enthralling
excitement of Mrs. Amorest's money. For days
now she had considered it, and with every day
and with every hour of every day the thing had
grown more dominating.

If that old woman was going to be left one

thousand pounds a year she would have some of it—a lot of it, half of it, more than half of it. The old woman was without a friend in the world, nor would she have a relation when her cousin died—you could not count that son of hers who, sure enough, had abandoned her for ever.

No; all that Agatha Payne had to do was to increase her influence, to make the old woman fond of her. Already she was fond of her; that was proved by the many occasions on which she came to visit her, but Agatha Payne must make her more fond of her. She must be very friendly and agreeable and neighbourly. . . . All day she had been forcing herself to be neighbourly, but her laziness was difficult to subdue. It was a cold day, although the sun was shining, and bed was very agreeable. As you went on through life, bed became more and more agreeable. But at last, around four in the afternoon, Agatha Payne had forced herself out slowly; as she washed and lazily put on a few clothes her brain crept round and round the thought of Lucy Amorest's money like a cat around a bird's cage.

She thought neither easily nor readily. Did she begin to think deeply, that pain bound itself about her head. She would sit before the old red tablecloth letting the cards slip through her fingers—knave of diamonds, four of hearts, queen of clubs, seven of hearts, three of clubs— and the fish would come swimming out of the green tank and would circle lazily about her head. Always she saw Lucy Amorest's money, like a fish larger than all the others and with dazzling scales of gold swimming just in front of her. She would put out her hand to touch it, but with a swerve of its tail it would be away, out of her reach, just above her head.

At last she became active enough to determine on a visit. She would go and see Lucy Amorest. So with a flick of her eye sending the fish back into the tank again and leaving the cards loose on the table under the guardianship of Miranda, she opened the door, shuffled across the hall, and knocked.

There was no answer from Mrs. Amorest's room. She knocked again. Still no answer. Where could the old woman be? She opened the door and looked in. No one there. She closed it and stood, licking her finger, considering. She would not be out, it was late now and dark. Ah, the other old lady, the new tenant!

And suddenly the fear struck her that perhaps this new tenant, this Miss Bellringer or whatever Mrs. Bloxam said her name was, might also have her designs on Lucy Amorest's money.

Lucy Amorest had told her—why then should she not also tell Miss Bellringer? Agatha Payne's face grew angry and troubled. Let them just try, those two! She'd show them! Already it seemed to her that she had a right to Lucy Amorest's money, to part of it at any rate. Let any one come in and deprive her of what was truly hers and she would show them!

It was with the sudden determination that they were at this very moment plotting together in there that she moved towards the third door farther down the passage (the one that had until lately concealed the life, hopes, and last torments of old red-faced Mr. Hopper, dead of double pneumonia) and knocked. Some one said "Come in," and she entered. It was immediately after that that the critical moment of her life came to her. She had been expecting to see nothing but two old women gossiping together; rather than that she saw, straight before her, as though it had been placed there for her special glory, the heart and centre of all the colour of the world.

The lamplight, the leaping fire illumined it.
Ruby and crimson and amber, blood red and
honey gold, threaded with flame and clouded
with smoky bronze, the pedestal and the dragon
came to her. From that instant of their mutual
greeting they were one. Far back, deep set in
her gipsy ancestry, she had been arrayed as a
queen and colour of flame and fire, and running
splendour had been her rightful dower.

Now she clutched her soiled wrapper about
her breasts and lusted for possession as never
in her lazy, sensuous, imaginative life she had
lusted before.

Mrs. Amorest, looking upwards, felt something strange in her gaze. It was strange that she
should be here at all. But she did the honours.
"Miss. Beringer," she said, "this is Mrs. Payne
who lives with us on this floor."

Agatha Payne came forward. Miss Beringer
awkwardly rose, and, as she always did when she
was nervous, giggled. Agatha Payne spoke in
her deep thick voice:

"I am glad to meet you."

"You'll have some tea, won't you?" said Miss
Beringer. "I'll fetch another cup. You must
want some tea, I'm sure. I'll get a cup in a

moment." She went to the cupboard and Agatha Payne settled down into the vacant chair, her eyes still on the mantelpiece.

"We've been to the Cathedral," said Mrs. Amorest amiably, "and we've enjoyed it so much. They had that anthem about the Wilderness that I always like. A boy sang so well. Have you been out, Mrs. Payne?"

"No, I have not." Mrs. Payne smiled and did her best to look amiable. "Now don't you go out overtiring yourself. It would never do for you to be knocked up. We can't have you ill."

"Oh, really," said Mrs. Amorest, laughing, "I am very well indeed. I never was better. I did feel a little bit tired when I first came in, but I'm quite rested now. Miss Beringer's tea has done me a world of good."

Miss Beringer had brought another cup and Mrs. Payne had her tea. Her chair was too small for her. She billowed around it. Her eyes never left the mantelpiece.

"That's a beautiful thing you have there," she said at last.

"Oh, my piece of amber," said Miss Beringer nervously. "Yes, that's my piece of amber, my most precious possession. It was given me years ago by my dearest friend. I'm so glad you like it."

"I do like it," said Mrs. Payne, breathing deeply and staring at it so fixedly that you might think that she hoped to draw it to her, magnet-wise. "I do like it."

"I'm so glad you do," said Miss Beringer. "It's been much admired. Every one likes it. They say I could get a great deal of money for it if I wished to sell it. It's worth a lot of money, I believe."

"Do you think you would sell it if you were offered a large sum?" asked Agatha Payne.

"Oh dear no!" said Miss Beringer. "Nothing would induce me. It was a present from my dearest friend. The greatest friend of my life gave it to me. I would never sell it. Nothing would induce me."

Agatha Payne slowly rose. Her knees were trembling with excitement. "May I look at it closer?" she asked.

"Why, certainly," said Miss Beringer. "Please do."

Agatha Payne went close to the mantelpiece.

something to be afraid of. I'm sure I don't like being under the same roof with her. She'll do something to me in my sleep."

Mrs. Amorest consoled her as best she could but in her heart was a little scorn for this silly, frightened woman, and a foreboding that she herself would have a tiresome time with such a companion. She said good-night kindly and, moved by her own good heart, bent forward and kissed the other's withered cheek.

"Don't you worry, dear," she said. "Have a good sleep and you'll find you won't be thinking of it in the morning."

But Miss Beringer did think of it. After Mrs. Amorest's departure she went to her door and locked it. Then she called Pip to her and sat with the dog straddled upon her lap, staring wide-eyed into the fading fire and every once and again giving a little shiver.

CHAPTER V

IT was a seasonable Christmas that year. Enough snow fell, then enough frost came, and then the sun shone. If it did not shine, at least it rode a circle of crimson fire through the heavens and, before the frost but after the slime of preparatory fogs, fragments of its fire splashed the High Street and spread in pools across the Precincts floor.

As I have intimated in other chronicles, Polchester of the old days was an enclosed town. The Riviera was unknown to it and the Garden of Allah a dream with Omar. Though London might call to the richer citizens on one occasion or another, at Christmas time every one stayed at home and, more wonderful yet to our modern disillusion, enjoyed family parties with Christmas trees, plum puddings, stockings, and the waits invited into the hall. It is not true, however, that the weather was any more romantic

then than it is to-day; there were just as many
rainy and muggy and foggy and dirty and dismal
skies, and Glebeshire, warmer than any other part
of the British Isles, has never had an intimate
acquaintance with crisp and shining snow. About
once in twenty years there are snowfalls, frosts,
and blue skies, and how happy then every one
is and how eagerly every one hands down the
year to an envious posterity!

This was such a year, and ten days before
Christmas the frost came and held, the powdered
snow remained jewelled and resplendent, the
sun looked down from a sky as delicately blue as
an egg-shell and laughed to see the fun. And
fun there was!

Magnet's toy-shop in the Market Cloisters
had a Father Christmas, a true and veritable
Father Christmas to be seen with two crimson
cheeks and long snow-white beard any afternoon
between two and four. Jeremy Cole so beheld
him, and his sisters Mary and Helen, and the
Dean's son Ernest, and the Fisher girls, and little
Tommy Chawner. He did not say much, but
he moved between the dolls and the trains, the
balls and the soldiers, as only Santa Claus could
move, with an authority, a benignity, a ripe wis-

dom that no impostor could have been clever enough to feign!

Every one did their best. In the Marketplace there was a Punch and Judy with a thickset jolly-faced man in charge, and he might have been that very same Garrick, friend of Maradick, whose history has been elsewhere narrated. I don't say he was, and I don't say he wasn't. Half-way up the High Street, Gummridge's the stationers had a whole Christmas tree in their window. Here was a stumbling-block to the whole High Street traffic. It was quite impossible to get any child—any perambulator baby indeed—past that window. It was a tree frosted, coloured, and shining, hung about with every glittering bauble, shaped to a perfect pinnacle of exquisite symmetry. But best of all was the window of Hunt & Griffin, the General Store, for here, for the first time in Polchester history, was a whole front window given over to pageantry, to none other than the scene in the life of Cinderella when, despondent beside the fire, she is amazed by the sudden apparition of her peaked-hatted Godmother. There is the fire and there Cinderella, there the pots and pans, the brick floor, and the huge kitchen rafters, there the Godmother, and there beyond the snow-lined window-pane the vision of the gold coach and the snow-white ponies. So great was the confusion outside the window that had this occurred in these traffic-haunted times the show must have been forbidden, but in those lucky days nobody minded, nobody cared. Let the children have a good time, Christmas comes but once a year, and even Mrs. Sampson, although her neuralgia was at its height, could not but admit that the window made a happy display.

The town rang during those days with laughter. Propter Hill outside the town had just enough snow on it to allow of tobogganing, and Pol Fields, having been flooded, gave for a whole wonderful fortnight the most marvellous skating. The town rang with laughter and the ringing of bells. The Cathedral let itself go and burst into perpetual peals of merriment to the great annoyance of late sleepers, dyspeptics, and ruminating essayists. There was fun everywhere, apples and oranges in the Market-place, and carols up and down the streets after dark.

It was the best Christmas that Polchester had known for many a day past or would know for many a day to come.

Mrs. Amorest was one who had always en-joyed a seasonable Christmas. To her as to every old person Christmas was filled with sad memo-ries, but she had a wonderful gift of enjoying fun at the moment of its occurrence, and being aware that she was so enjoying it, and because the fun in her life had been neither frequent nor extrava-gant very small occurrences amused and excited her.

This was the happiest Christmas known to her for many a day. Struggle as she might not to think of the money coming to her, she could not keep it out of her consciousness. She told herself again and again (and when she was alone in her room she repeated the words aloud sometimes) that she must not place too strong a reliance on her cousin's promise. "He may have altered his mind the next moment. It's silly to believe him." Nevertheless the solemnity of his words, the caress of his hand as it rested on her head—these things were difficult to dismiss.

And the happiness that came from the promise was also difficult to dismiss. She was naturally happy. Give her the least excuse and she must be happy. Although she believed that God did not intend that human beings should be very happy because they were in this world for the training of their souls, and souls were better trained by sorrow than by joy, nevertheless an imp of happiness would continue to jump in her heart and stir her little world with his discordant cries of joy. Joy at what? A kindly action, a splash of sun across the street, a barrel-organ round the corner, a stained-glass window, an apple, and a piece of cheese. She *could* not keep down her spirits as, being a penniless, lonely old widow of over seventy, she should.

And, this Christmas, she lost completely her self-control. She adored above everything else in the world the spending of money, perhaps for the very reason that she never had very much to spend. She had never been able to believe that statement often written in the papers that millionaires did not know what to do with their money. Did not know! Why, she could spend a million pounds quite easily at Gummridge's alone! But there! The newspapers were never to be trusted. She liked greatly to be given things, but still better was it herself to make presents. The excitement of giving some one something he or she wanted was intense, to watch the opening of the parcel, to see the stare of pleasure and surprise, to hear the exclamation, to feel the affection flowing out—was there any luxury in life like it?

And it was a luxury that, of late, she had been compelled to deny herself. Last Christmas she had given Agatha Payne half a dozen pocket-handkerchiefs, Mrs. Bloxam a piece of ribbon, and her cousin a pocket-book. Worst sorrow of all, it was impossible to send Brand anything. No use to throw parcels out into the void. The best she could do was to write two letters, one a month in advance, and this she sent to the only address she had, something in California, and then one on Christmas Eve, such as she had always written to him at Christmas time. This she also sent out to California, but she wrote it because for a moment it brought him closer to her—she felt, with his photograph up there in front of her, as though she had him with her in the room. These were all but poor substitutes for reality, and, cheat ourselves as we may, our subconscious selves refuse to be deceived. Mrs. Amorest knew nothing about her subconscious self, but she did know that after last Christmas she had a miserable sense of inadequacy and frustrated purpose. She had made nobody happy. Even Mrs. Bloxam had disappeared into the intimacies of her family to emerge two days later with a black eye and a bruised cheek. This year she would fling her cap over the mill. She had prospects. She did not face them finally, those prospects, did not take them, hold them in front of her, look them in the eyes and say to them as one always ought to do to prospects, "Now, are you sound and healthy? Have you got heart and lungs and legs and arms and a good stiff back?" No, she merely reported on them—she heard that they were good and healthy and promised very well indeed! Then she went ahead.

The plan came to her in the middle of the night, or rather in one of those early morning hours when the first cock crows and the hidden despair raises its abominable head. Lying there in the early morning she drove her despairs away and considered Miss Beringer. Poor Miss Beringer! What a frightened, nervous, trembling creature she was! She would like to do something for her! She would like well to give her a happy Christmas! And Agatha Payne, too. It was then that the idea came to her.

At first she was frightened of it. It would

demand energy and persistence. And *had* she money enough? Money in the future would not do. She examined her purse and found that she had sufficient did she use part of next quarter's rent. She trembled at that, but she was sure that kind Mr. Agnew, when he knew of the promise that her cousin had made to her, would not hesitate to advance her. . . .

She trembled. Her heart warned her. Her cheeks were flushed and she had a guilty air. But she held to her purpose, and once she had begun she did not look back. Once she had begun she *could* not look back. She moved, during those frosty coloured days, about the town, the very spirit of adventure. She found that she must go quietly. The excitement tired her, and sometimes she would, in a moment, feel so weary that she *could* not get to the top of the High Street, and on one occasion when she was at the top she could not go down again and had to take refuge in the shop of Mr. Bennett, the grand bookseller. There she sat, greatly alarmed, on a chair in the very middle of the shop with busts of Byron and Walter Scott looking down on her and a grand smell of Russian leather and old vellum in her nostrils, and the complete works of George Eliot at her elbow. Old Mr. Bennett was very kind to her although she told him at once that she was not there to buy anything, and who should come in at that very moment but Archdeacon Brandon himself, magnificent, handsome, superb, ordering somebody "on the Psalms" with the air of a king and a conqueror. She looked around her with the hope of seeing some of her husband's plays, and when she did not would have liked to ask Mr. Bennett whether he kept them in stock, but her courage failed her and she could only thank him very much and slip out of the shop as quietly as possible. Fortunately she did not hear the Archdeacon's question: "And who was that shabby little woman?" He asked out of all kindness, feeling it his duty as the father of the flock to keep his eye upon all the inhabitants of the town.

She tried to keep her head about her purchases. She found, as many another has found before and after her, that the best things were always the most expensive. And then when it came to the central purchase of all, to the core, the heart, the kernel, the pinnacle, the *pièce de résistance*, the *raison d'être*, and any other foreign phrase that you prefer, she found that *here* expense was inevitable. Try as you would, it must cost more than you had supposed. Of course she only wanted a small one, but even the small ones. . . . And then at the last, two days before Christmas, she found in the Market-place, in a corner behind the old woman under the green umbrella, the very thing, a darling, a perfect specimen, a miracle, and, when she enquired of the nice round-faced man whose possession it was, she found that it was only . . . well, less than the experience of the last two days had led her to believe possible, although more, a good deal more, than she had originally intended. She bought it, and ordered that it should be sent to her room, blushing a little in spite of herself as she named the address. She gave her name very carefully, begging him to be watchful that it should not be sent to any other room by mistake, and he promised her, saying that he would himself bring it.

He did in fact arrive with it when she was there, and she liked him very much, holding him in conversation for quite a while, and then giving him an orange for the baby. After that she guarded her room like a dragoness and would not allow May Beringer, who was already forming a too constant habit of "dropping in," to cross her threshold.

Christmas Eve arrived, and Mrs. Amorest, awaking to the inspiring voice of Mrs. Bloxam, was delighted when she discovered how fine and clear it was; no wind, the smoke rising from the chimneys elephant grey against the blue, the thin rind of frost, the sparrows already chattering at her window for their crumbs.

After her little mid-day meal she sat down to the table, found her paper and envelopes, and wrote to Brand.

Her letter was as follows:

MY DEAREST, DARLING BOY—I must write to you as I always do, although I sadly fear that it will be a long time before you get this letter. The one that I wrote to you a month ago may reach you before Christmas, and I hope it will. This I am writing because it seems as though I am talking to you, and I don't wish to allow Christmas to pass by without having a word with my dear boy.

Perhaps you have been writing to me and still to the old address. I told them in Cheltenham to forward anything on, but they are so stupid at the post-office, although, as a matter of fact, I always think it wonderful, considering the sort of postmen one sees walking about, that they don't lose more letters than they do—quite boys some of them are, and they none of them have very intelligent faces, although I daresay they are good men.

Well, dearest boy, I try to imagine to myself the kind of Christmas you are having, but it is really difficult for me, because you told me in the last letter I had from you that it was quite hot at Christmas time. That seems to me very strange and not very nice, I think. Of course it is often warm here for Christmas. Both last year and the year before that we had rain and muggy weather, but this year it is delightful, with a hard frost and the sun shining, cold and seasonable. It's so pleasant for the children and more healthy for everybody, I am sure.

I am very well in health. That cough I had when I wrote to you last has quite gone away and I am sure it's those lozenges that I found at Cubitt's (he's our best chemist here in the High Street). If only I could hear that you are quite well and will come home soon for a visit I would be quite happy. You know, dear boy, I am an old woman now and can't expect to live for ever, so that I do hope you'll be able to come home soon. It's very nice here and I'm very comfortable. There's something else I'd like to tell you about, but I suppose that I must not just yet because it isn't quite settled. I think of you so much and pray for you night and morning. At this time of the year when God came down to earth and took upon Him our flesh and was a little baby in a manger, I think we should all make Him feel how thankful we are. I know that He is looking after you and so I don't worry about you. At least I know that you are warm. You used to be so careless about your under-clothing when you were a little boy.

My dearest boy, you are always in my thoughts.— Your loving   MOTHER.

She sat for a long time after she had written the letter with his photograph in front of her. She thought of him in all the ways that she had known him—as a baby at her breast, as a small boy in his first trousers, as a boy going to his first

day-school and forgetting her so quickly in the
new excitements of other boys and games and
masters, as all right and proper boys must do, of
course. And then, as he grew, her interest in the
strange new personality that developed, as flower
from the bud—a personality that was so strange
because it was like neither herself nor his father,
somebody quite new. And then his growing independence, his chafing at the literary and artistic
interests of his father, his desire for the open-air
life and complete independence. Then her own
strange sympathy with him; and although she
loved him so dearly she understood that he should
want to get away and be free. She had felt it
herself in her married life, and she realised that
he *was* her own son, not by right of the quiet and
domestic character that was most obvious in her,
but by right of that secret independence and
sharpness of judgment that her married life had
subdued in her. He left her and at intervals
returned to her. She had been a woman of forty
when she had borne him, and he had been only
twenty-seven when she had last seen him, still a
boy although so strong and independent! She
looked at the photograph until she seemed to
draw him out of the frame and he came to her

and put his arms round her and teased her in the old laughing way that he had always had. But she was not simply a sentimental woman; she was in fact scornful of emotion that led to nothing, and so she put the photograph back upon the mantelpiece, put on her bonnet and her coat, and, because it was already three o'clock and would soon be dusk, hurried off to take her present to her cousin.

This year she was giving him a picture, a photogravure in a nice black frame of Holman Hunt's "Carpenter's Shop." She had not been quite lately to visit him lest she should seem to be reminding him of his promise. She had not heard how his health was, but she hoped that this bright weather had helped him, and that he would perhaps see her. Nevertheless as she crossed the bridge and climbed the hill a little chilling wind, whence she knew not, breathed upon her heart. Rising out of the dark purple-hued river appeared the figure of Agatha Payne.

She saw, quite unexpectedly, reasons for May Beringer's terrors. There *was* something alarming about Agatha, something not quite normal and healthy, something odd and twisted. It came, perhaps, because the poor old thing lived

so much alone, but Mrs. Amorest gave a little
shiver and thought to herself that she would
move from that house in the spring to somewhere brighter and more companionable. She
could not drive the company of Agatha from her
mind. All up the hill it kept pace with her, and
then, in another flash of memory, she saw a picture of her childhood, something that had not
come to her for many a year. It was a picture
that used to hang in the dining-room, of a witch
weaving her spells in a dark and lonely wood.
Before her was a large iron pot into which she
flung toads and snakes and strange purple-tinted
leaves. From the cauldron came a blue thick
smoke. It was true that the witch did not physically resemble Agatha. She was old and skinny,
with a back bent double and long groping fingers,
but there was something . . . something. . . .

And then, pausing for breath before she
entered her cousin's gate, she smiled at her folly.
Her practical mind drove her fancies like mist
into the frosty air.

The house, always ugly and forbidding, seemed
simply not to belong to the fresh and wonderful
day. The woods that fringed the hill were marvellous in their mystery, the fragments of the

river that gleamed among the brown folds of the sloping fields glittered like shreds of broken glass faintly amethyst, the powdered frost shone and twinkled in the sharp and friendly air, but the house was untouched by this beauty; aloof and hostile it seemed to deride and despise any spirit that could wish goodwill to men and friendship to all the world. To Mrs. Amorest especially, as she approached it, it seemed to say: "You aren't truly so sentimental as to believe that the human race is loving and kind. Rid yourself of your illusions. You should be ashamed of yourself at your age that you have any."

As she rang the bell and heard it clang defiantly through the house she felt again a dim and unhappy foreboding. She always disliked her meeting with the housekeeper. She felt that that woman despised and patronised her, and now to-day she wished that she might encounter no one who raised hostility in her heart. But one could only pass to her cousin over the housekeeper's body. There was no other way for it.

The woman herself opened the door and was more forbidding than she had ever been. Mrs. Amorest suspected that in some way she had learnt about her cousin's promise. Always before

there had been a tacit recognition, however reluc-
tant, that Mrs. Amorest had some right there.
To-day she blocked the doorway with her peevish
ill-natured body and showed no sign at all of
moving.   Mrs. Amorest felt a sudden, almost
affectionate, pity for her gift.   It had cost, as it
seemed to her, a large sum, but in the eyes of
this woman it would be simply another whee-
dling attempt on her part to extort more money
from her cousin.   She summoned her courage and
smiled her friendliest smile.

"Good afternoon.   How is my cousin to-day?"

"Not at all well, I'm afraid."

"Oh dear, I am sorry to hear that.   I thought
that this fine weather might have done him some
good."

There was no answer to this, so after a little
pause Mrs. Amorest, feeling the chill of the afternoon air, said:

"Of course it *is* cold, isn't it, but I thought
that, being in bed, he might not notice it.   Has
the doctor been to-day?"

"Yes, the doctor has been."

Well, she might ask me into the hall, thought
Mrs. Amorest.   "Could I see him for a moment,
do you think?"

"I'm afraid not, Mrs. Amorest. It was the doctor's orders that he was not to be disturbed."

"Not for a moment? I really would not bother him. Just to wish him a happy Christmas."

"I'm afraid not. Those were the doctor's orders."

"Would you not ask him whether he would not see me for a moment?"

"I'm sorry, but he is not to be disturbed by anybody."

There was a pause, and then Mrs. Amorest said cheerfully: "Oh, well, I'm sure that's quite right if the doctor says so. I only wanted to wish him a happy Christmas. I have a little gift." She produced it from under her arm. "I have written a little note in case I should not be able to see him. Would you kindly give it to him?"

"Certainly."

She took the parcel, looking neither at it nor at Mrs. Amorest, but forward into the brown and naked garden with a frown of determination as though she were forewarning some plant that was whispering hopefully about the spring that she was not going to stand any of that sort of nonsense.

There was another little pause, then Mrs. Amorest said: "Would you most kindly wish him a very happy Christmas for me? Of course I know that it can't be a *very* happy Christmas for him as ill as he is, but I always think it makes a difference if one knows that people are thinking of one, don't you?"

"I will certainly tell him."

"And I hope you'll have a happy Christmas too," said Mrs. Amorest, trembling with the cold, and wishing altogether in spite of her better feelings that the woman should herself know what it was to be kept out of a warm house on a cold day.

"Thank you very much, Mrs. Amorest. I wish you the same, I'm sure."

That was all. There was nothing more to be done. The door closed with a horrible final clang, and in some strange flash of vision she knew that she was never to enter that house again.

She walked down the hill, and in spite of all her courage, forebodings now crowded upon her. It was true that it was not her cousin's fault that he had not seen her. He had not known that she was there. But surely she had been foolish to build upon his idle word! And that woman. She had designs. She certainly had designs. She had looked at Mrs. Amorest with a hostility that could mean only one thing. And a sick man was so helpless, the worse his sickness the weaker he was. . . . As she crossed the bridge over the Pol it seemed to her that in another moment her courage would desert her. Because if that money did not come to her!

She summoned all her pluck, standing for a moment on the bridge and watching the river take on its evening colour, softly purple under the dark shadow of the rising hills.

Then, thinking of the evening that was coming and the fun that it would be, she smiled. Things always turned out better than you expected. The stars that were now breaking into the sky above her head were the eyes of God. She was watched over and cared for and protected. She had no need to fear.

The town as she passed up through the High Street was bubbling with merriment and gaiety. The shops blazed with lights; the street was crowded; every one was laughing and happy, hurrying along loaded with parcels, stopping to speak, it seemed, to any one who was near that they might wish them good luck. This was the world that Mrs. Amorest loved. Why might it not always be like this? She stopped at the Cinderella window. How pretty and touching! She turned round to a stout man beside her and said, "Isn't it pretty?"

"Indeed it is, mum," he answered her, smiling. "My little girl wants to take it home. Don't you, Pansy?" and a diminutive child squeaked out "Yes."

"What a pretty little girl!" said Mrs. Amorest.

"Thank you, mum," answered the fat man. "A merry Christmas, I'm sure."

"And the same to you," said Mrs. Amorest.

The rest of the way home seemed easy.

Arrived in her room, she set about the development of her plan. She had asked Agatha Payne and May Beringer to come and visit her at eight o'clock. She had two hours for her preparations. The time flashed by and in a moment it was a quarter to eight. She hurriedly put on her silk dress, hung around her neck her thin gold chain with the locket that held Brand's portrait, brushed her lovely white hair, put on her lace cap fresh and crisp from the laundry, then her stiff white cuffs. Finished. Completed. She sat down to survey her work. A smile played about her lips. It was the most beautiful thing that she had ever seen in her life.

At five minutes past eight there was a knock on her door, and then another knock. Agatha Payne and May Beringer entered. They stood bewildered on the threshold.

It was indeed a pretty sight. The curtains were drawn and the far end of the room was duskily shadowed, but at the fireplace end stood —THE TREE!

And what a tree! Of just the right size for the room, it had a shape and symmetry that surely no other tree in all Christmasdom could equal. It tapered gradually with exquisite shape and form to a point that quivered and flickered like a green flame. On the flame sturdily triumphed Father Christmas, diminutive in body, but alive in his smile, his stolidity, his gallant colour. It was the colour that entranced the eye. Mrs. Amorest had worked with the soul of an artist. She had not over-burdened the slender branches. The thin chains of frosted silver that hung from bough to bough seemed of themselves to dance in patterned rhythm. Balls of fire, emerald and ruby, amethyst and crystal, shone in the light of the candles. And at every place colour blended with colour. The tree was always the tree. The light that flashed from its boughs was not foreign to it, but seemed to be, integrally, part of its life and history. It had been placed on a long and broad looking-glass, into which it looked down as though into a lake of crystal water. The candles seemed to be the voices of the tree; it was vocal in its pleasure, its sense of fun at its own splendour, its grand surprise that after all it had come off so well.

In proportion, in blending of colour, in grandeur of spirit, it was the finest tree in England that night. On either side of the tree were two tables spread with white cloths. On one table were some parcels beautifully tied with coloured ribbons, and on the other sandwiches, a plum-cake with white icing, some saffron buns, and a dish of sweets and chocolates.

The two ladies stood amazed. So pretty was the room with its soft pink colours, its light dim save for the aureole of golden splendour shed by the tree, so utterly unexpected the display, that words would not come; only at last May Beringer cried, "Oh dear! Dear me! Dear me!"

Both ladies had dressed in their party best; May in her orange silk, that suited her, I fear, not too well, and Agatha in her dark purple, a dress of a fashion now forgotten, too small for her, but that nevertheless with her black hair finely brushed, her dark eyes flashing, gave her the air of older days, the air that had made Mr. Payne, thirty-five years ago, call her his "Gipsy Queen."

"Oh, I do hope you won't both think me too silly," said Mrs. Amorest, coming forward, "but I simply had to do something this Christmas. We've just done nothing the last two Christmasses and it did seem too bad. Don't you think so? I do hope you don't mind?"

"Mind?" said May Beringer, coming towards the tree and gazing at it with her mouth open like a school-girl. "Why, Mrs. Amorest, it's lovely! It's the loveliest thing! Why, I can't speak. I can't, indeed. Words won't come. I can't say anything at all."

Agatha Payne was moved more deeply still. The colour possessed her as colour always possessed her, coming towards her like a living breathing person, holding out its arms to her, whispering to her, "You and I! We are the only ones here who understand. I have been waiting for you, and you alone."

Indeed it seemed to her that the tree belonged to her and was hers absolutely. The two other women vanished from her consciousness; she could see only the pale golden flame of the candles, so steady, so pure, so dignified, the balls of amethyst and ruby and crystal as they swung and turned and gleamed so slightly and yet always with a secret life and purpose of their own.

And the deep green of the tree, richly velvet under the light of the candles! She stood absorbed, entranced, waves of sensuous pleasure running through her body.

So silent were they both that after a minute had passed Mrs. Amorest was alarmed.

"I'm so glad you like it," she said almost timidly. "Shan't we sit down and look at it? I like to think of all the other trees there are tonight in everybody's homes and the children dancing round them and the presents——"

She broke off because a longing for Brand came to her so urgently that it was all she could do not to call out his name. For a moment it seemed to her foolish humbug, sham, and ridiculous sentiment, that the three of them, old, forgotten, not wanted by anybody, should indulge in this display. But looking up at the tree she was comforted. Anything so beautiful had its own purpose. She had made a beautiful thing. She felt the joy of the creator in her handiwork.

They sat in a row looking at the tree. May Beringer was, all in a moment, voluble. She had so much to tell them,—of the trees that she had known, the trees that she had had in her own house, the trees that she and Jane Betts had decorated together, the Christmas festivities that they had had in Exeter (you would think to hear her that Exeter was the centre of all the splendour and gaiety of the world). Oh! she talked and laughed and was so wildly excited that she nearly cried.

Agatha Payne said very little. She only stared and stared at the tree.

The next part of the entertainment arrived. Mrs. Amorest picked up the parcels in their lovely white paper and coloured ribbon and, blushing a little (shell pink faintly colouring the ivory of her cheeks), said:

"These are little tiny things that I got. You

mustn't laugh at me, please, for getting them. I think the chief part of a present is that it should be wrapped up in paper, don't you? But I hope you'll like them."

And they did like them. At least May Beringer liked hers. She had a case with three pairs of scissors and a book in a purple cover, *The Light of Asia*, by Sir Edwin Arnold. Agatha Payne said little about hers—only "Thank you, Lucy," in a deep hoarse-throated murmur. She had a box of coloured cottons and a purple blotter. She could not take her eyes away from the tree.

Then they cut the cake and ate the sandwiches, and Mrs. Amorest made tea and listened happily, cosily to May Beringer's reminiscences.

How happy it was with the blazing tree, the dim room, the bells pealing beyond the window, the crackling fire!

Each old lady forgot the other. They were lost in their own world of remembered and recaptured life,—past joys, past sorrows, past desires, past regrets. The clock ticked on, the candles burnt with steady flame, the bells rang out.

Gradually Lucy Amorest closed her eyes. She heard May Beringer's voice from a vast distance.

Then her own faintly replying, "How curious! Indeed . . . In . . . deed."

Her head sank upon her breast. May Beringer also, bathed in the warmth of the room, comforted with tea and happiness, closed her eyes. Her head nodded—once and twice and thrice. She pulled herself up. Stared sharply at Mrs. Amorest. Saw two Mrs. Amorests, then three. Her head fell. She also slept.

Only Agatha Payne, her dark eyes fixed, sat, without moving, staring at the tree.

CHAPTER VI

AGATHA SECRETLY . . .

O N the following evening Agatha Payne entered Mrs. Amorest's room and asked her whether she would light the tree again. She did so, but the candles were now very low. They flickered up in wild and despairing flares. One caught a branch and must at once be extinguished. The two ladies sat there watching the death of the tree. It was Christmas night and very silent. The ladies said very little to one another, and at last Agatha Payne with a husky "Good-night," vanished.

Agatha's soul was like a house of many stories. In youth she had lived in the top story, attic in shape but with a truly fine view from the windows. Here there had been light, air, and fine prospects. Then as the years passed she moved down on to the middle floor, where she was exercised about the furniture of the bedroom and held, elegant receptions in the drawing-room. After the middle years she moved definitely on to the ground floor, and lived during a great part of her time in the dining-room nibbling at the crystallised cherries, squeezing the pears on their china dish, and slipping into her mouth the chocolate almonds. There was no view from the dining-room windows.

But the first time she stumbled down over the dark stone steps into the cellars was one day after her husband's death, when her sister-in-law came to visit her. She hated her sister-in-law because her sister-in-law was afraid of her. She hated and despised her, so she pushed her down the cellar steps in front of her, made her scream, showed her the dank, dark place, and hauled her up again. For herself, she saw that there were things in the cellar that interested her—rows of dusty wine-bottles, spiders' webs, and broken furniture. She came to live down there almost entirely. Of course, here there was no view at all.

This was her own house and nobody else lived in it at all, but in the house in Pontippy Square there were several other lodgers.

Living deep in her own cellar with her fish and her coloured cards, she had not been until now aware of the life beyond her. Lucy Amorest a shade, and behind that shadow others yet more shadowy.

She was vaguely conscious of desires, but deep down in her cellar she had grown unaccustomed to the full light. She was uncertain of the division between reality and unreality. Nor did she greatly care.

Old people, when they are happy and contented, are the spectators of life. They sit and watch with smiles on their faces, and hands happily folded. But let them feel that they have not had enough out of life, that life has treated them ill, that there is still time to snatch a valuable or two, and they will plunge into the mêlée, cap awry, hair disordered, and will, as likely as not, make a pretty scene of terror and dismay before Death with his bony fingers leads them out of the battle.

Agatha Payne had for many a day now been a spectator only of her own emotions and atmosphere; now in a flash the thin bony body of May Beringer and her piece of red amber were in front of her, tugging at her, dragging her out of her lethargy and idleness, possessing all that was left of her imagination and lustful desires.

It was after that Christmas Eve and the lighting of the tree that the whole forces of her spirit began once again to move. She thirsted for a continuation of that pleasure that was so sharp in its apprehension that it was a lust. She wanted something; she must have it; she must have that piece of red amber. She must have it not only because she wished that her eyes should be able to rest on it whenever they desired to do so, but also because she wished that it should be hers, hers body and soul; she wanted that response from it that you only get when you are master. She wished that when she put her hands about its cold smooth surface she could feel that its heart was beating at her touch, and that it knew that it belonged to her and to her alone.

She must have it, and she would get it, because Mrs. Amorest (who was coming into money and would be very rich) would buy it for her from May Beringer.

And if May Beringer would not sell it? Here began the second impulse of her excitement. She had, at the first view, not disliked the woman. She had had no very active feelings concerning her. Then she had perceived that the woman was afraid of her.

As the rabbit is to the snake, as the sparrow is to the hawk, as the mouse is to the cat, so was timidity to Agatha Payne. She was not, take her life from first to last, a cruel woman. She had, in the first periods of it, done kindly actions. She could admire, she understood loyalty, she remembered brave deeds. But did any one cringe to her, did she detect fear in the eyes raised to her, then a savage satisfaction warmed her heart and the stir of persecution crept into her eyes. Even then she did not actually intend cruelty. She felt a scorn for any coward, and when, added to the scorn, there was irritation, it was natural enough that it should be sharp and contemptuous. After that curiosity had led her forward. Was anybody so true a coward as that? Could their fear lead them to such subterfuges? If she did this, would their action be that? Of what stuff *could* they be made?

That was in her younger days. For a number of years now she had not moved sufficiently into the outer world to encounter new personalities— neither Mrs. Amorest nor Mrs. Bloxam feared her.

She was also moving in her cellar ever deeper and deeper into the dusk. It was hard for her to see now because of the shadows. Her curiosity was less active than her desire to satisfy her thirsts and hungers. When she lusted for the red amber it was because she wished to draw it into herself. She sat like a spider lazily in the centre of a web that had grown up around her rather than been actually created by her. She would draw May Beringer into the centre of it and eat her up did she not let her have that piece of red amber.

But she bore May Beringer no ill-will. She only lazily despised her.

Then as the days passed her consciousness was aroused more actively and she began to hate her. She hated her for the noise that her slippers made, for the way that she sniffed and would not use her handkerchief, but especially for her nervous "Bye-bye" with which she always ended their meetings.

"Bye-bye," "Bye-bye," "Bye-bye," bleating like a sheep. And what a thing for a lady to say, and, if say it she must, why not bravely and with spirit instead of that timid, unctuous eagerness?

Agatha, back in her room after a visit, would stand looking at her fish, at Miranda, and the

cards, would stamp her foot and mutter "Bye-bye
—Bye-bye. Bye-bye. Idiot!"

She hated, too, May Beringer's dog, as crawling and sycophantic as its mistress. She stood
glowering at it, casting spells over it, wishing it
evil; and the dog knew standing there, with its
head down, shivering, giving her once and again
a supplicating glance.

So during these wet, muggy January days she
made it her habit to pay May Beringer visits.
She went because the red amber irresistibly drew
her. She must see it every day, and if possible
twice a day. And soon she went because she
wished to see that terrified glance flash into May
Beringer's eyes. She liked to see it there. It
should be there permanently before she had done
with her.

Old Mrs. Payne was looking, Mrs. Bloxam
declared, ten years younger.

On the other hand, she did not forget Lucy
Amorest; or perhaps, to speak truly, Lucy
Amorest's money. She was vague about Mrs.
Amorest's money as she was about everything in
the outside world. Some one must die before
it became Mrs. Amorest's, but somebody would
die very soon. She had only to look at the cards,

to allow them to trickle through her fingers, to rattle on to the table, to perceive clearly how soon somebody would die. . . .

And then there was the old woman with more money than she could use.

She would appear at Mrs. Amorest's door, tall and shapeless and silent. Staring. It was generally in the early dusk of the winter afternoon, and often in these days the rain tickled the window-panes and rustled about the coals. Mrs. Amorest would be reading her book. She would look up and see the tall old woman there.

She was not afraid of Mrs. Payne, but since she had realised May Beringer's alarm she had been aware of a sort of uncertainty, a discomfort, a hesitation. She felt now a purpose in Agatha Payne's visits. The woman was after something. But what? There was nothing that Mrs. Amorest had that *could* attract her. And yet there she was, wanting something.

She wished, too, to be friendly. When Mrs. Amorest looked up she saw her leaning against the post of the door, smiling in a grim, strange way.

"Come and sit down, dear," Mrs. Amorest would say, laying her book on the table, and in her lumping, clumsy fashion Agatha Payne would shift to a chair and overflow into it. On a certain January afternoon of storm and rain, it seemed that she had made up her mind to something. She stared with her motionless black eyes for some while before speaking, then at last she broke out:

"How's your cousin, Lucy?"

Mrs. Amorest, startled, raised her snow-white head. "My cousin?"

"Yes. The one who's dying and leaving you his money?"

"Oh, Agatha, I don't know whether he's really leaving me his money. I oughtn't to have said anything about it."

"Nonsense," Agatha's voice rumbled out. "Why shouldn't you say something? If he promised it to you, he promised it to you."

"But he didn't promise it. He was only being kind for the moment. And I've never seen him since. I am afraid that he is very ill indeed. I do wish that I could see him. He has a housekeeper who doesn't like me, I'm afraid."

"Oh, doesn't she?" Agatha's eyes stared. "Why doesn't she?"

"I don't know. I don't think I like her either."

"But he did promise it to you?"

"Yes."

"He said that when he died——?"

Mrs. Amorest broke in: "Agatha, don't you think there's something rather dreadful in our talking about money like this, when we're both so old? You know we're both over seventy, and although we don't talk of it often, nor think of it either perhaps, yet some time one must remember that one can only have a few more years to live. Aren't you ever afraid of death, Agatha?"

Agatha Payne raised her head as though she were trying to see more distinctly through the dusk of a darkening room.

"We can have twenty years yet," she said hoarsely. "You're strong and I'm strong. Mrs. Bloxam had a little girl who died when she was five. What's the good of thinking about it?"

"We ought to think of it, I'm sure," said Mrs. Amorest vigorously. "Not in an unwholesome way, of course, but as though we were going from one country into another. And we must give an account of ourselves. God will know all, and if it were not for His infinite mercy our danger would be great indeed. His love—I like to think of His love."

There was a long silence between them. The coals clicked in the grate. The rain stroked the windows. At last Agatha Payne said, "What would you do with the money, Lucy, if you did get it?"

"Do with it?" Mrs. Amorest started. She had been dreaming. "I should find my boy and make him comfortable."

"Oh, your boy!" Mrs. Payne snorted. "Would you lend me some of it?"

"Lend you some? Why, of course."

Mrs. Payne smiled. "You're a good creature, Lucy. But I'd do the same for you. Have you seen Miss Beringer's fine coloured piece on the mantelpiece?"

"That pretty thing! Yes, I told her how greatly I admired it."

"I don't know what an old woman like her is doing with it. She can't appreciate it."

"She likes it," said Mrs. Amorest, "because her greatest friend gave it to her, and that's a very good reason."

Agatha Payne got up. She yawned. Then she shuffled to the door. She seemed already to have forgotten her companion. She went without speaking.

But that night she asked May Beringer to come in and drink a cup of tea with her. May Beringer came, although dearly would she have liked to refuse.

For one thing, she hated old Mrs. Payne's room. It smelt to her "graveyardy." She was sure that the windows were never opened. For another, Pip would not pass that threshold. Not that Mrs. Payne wanted him to do so; she hated the dog, and quite frankly said so. But the dog would not have gone had all the bones and biscuits from the dogs' Paradise been held in front of his nose. His terror of Mrs. Payne was something curious to witness and dreadfully distressing to his mistress, who had never seen him like that with any one before. Long before the old woman's tall figure appeared in the doorway he knew that she was coming. He would raise his head. His eyes would sharpen, his gaze would be fixed on the door. When she entered he would crawl under the chair. His spirit would be broken by her presence.

All this did not cause May Beringer herself to like the lady the better. But she was in any case a weak creature, and when she was afraid, she was pitiful.

We are so largely the playthings of Fate in our fears. To one, fear of the dark, to another of physical pain, to a third of public ridicule, to a fourth of poverty, to a fifth of loneliness—for all of us our own particular creature lurks in ambush. Nor is it our choice of place or creature.

There was nothing in the world that May Beringer did not fear, but behind all her terrors there was a strange determined obstinacy. As a girl at school it had been discovered by other girls that you could terrify, torture, have all the fun of your life by resolved and calculated persecution, and then, in a moment when you least expected it, up would come this obstinacy, this martyr determination. Often enough some tiny thing called it forth. She would yield with shrieks of terror to demand after demand, and then at the last, over a pin, a cloud in the sky, a falling leaf, she would stand up and act Joan the Martyr to the end of time.

It depends, after all, on what you have in your eye. For one it is a seat in the House of Parliament, for another a lop-eared rabbit, for another a ship at sea, for another a shadow on a green field, for another quails in aspic, for few the welcoming light in a friend's eye, for fewer yet the resting of God's hand upon the shoulder . . . for May Beringer it was the memory of Jane Betts.

Here her brain moved curiously, because in some odd way she connected Agatha Payne with Jane. Because she never analysed anything she did not track this down, but dimly in her distressed mind it came to this, that Agatha Payne wanted to take Jane away from her. But that was absurd, because Agatha scarcely knew that Jane had ever existed. And yet there it was. That was the way that May felt about it.

She realised that Agatha Payne was paying her visits twice daily, and that there was some reason for these. She did not as yet connect them with the piece of red amber.

She had been twice to Mrs. Payne's room and against her will. She had felt quite faint there, as though some one were trying to strangle her. She had hated the gloom, the half light, the green picture with the fish.

She never knew what to say to Mrs. Payne. She trickled a conversation on ordinary occasions, but here words deserted her. She always felt at her worst here and overwhelmed with apprehension. Apprehension of everything, but especially

of being without any money at all, quite alone in
the world, dying of starvation, forgotten, in the
room in Pontippy Square. Sitting in Mrs. Payne's
room she would see this vision and twist her bony
hands together on her lap, struggling with the
agony of it.

She could not think why this old woman asked
her to come when she disliked her as she did.
Disliked her! There was never any question of
that; the malevolent look that she caught sometimes in Mrs. Payne's eye was witness enough.

To-night Mrs. Payne showed more plainly
than ever she had done before her intentions. She
brewed the tea, very strong and dark, laid out
the two plates with the sweet biscuits, and then,
sitting up at the table and letting the cards fall
through her fingers, said:

"I don't want to be impertinent, Miss Beringer,
but do tell me of your plans."

"Oh, I don't know," said May Beringer, crack-
ing and uncracking her fingers, "I really don't
know. It's so difficult to say, isn't it? How
can one truly know? I hope to find some work
very shortly."

"What kind of work?" asked Mrs. Payne.

"Companion to some lady, perhaps. Some old

lady, you know, who can't look after herself.
Some one too old to really care for herself."

"These old women," thought Agatha Payne.
"Strange creatures. Never realise they are old.
Lucy Amorest just the same. Think they'll go
on for ever." She looked at May Beringer in her
faded green dress and cheap string of coral beads,
with her untidy hair and large nose, and was, at
that glance, so strangely irritated that two of the
fish came out of the tank and swam slowly, lazily
about the room. She would like to do that silly
old woman a mischief, apart altogether from the
piece of red amber. Yes, she would. She would
like to put her rough strong hands about that
skinny neck and squeeze it. Oh, she would! She
offered May Beringer another sweet biscuit and
said, kicking her heel in the air:

"But those jobs are rather hard to find, you
know—and you're not as strong as you were."

May Beringer, at the bare mention of the
words, felt a shoot of pain through her limbs, and
said:

"No, that's quite true. But I'm very hale and
hearty still. Still quite strong. If the work
were not too arduous. . . ."

"Would you sell that piece of red amber you have, if things went badly?"

"Oh no. I shouldn't like to sell that. I shall never sell it. It was given to me by my best friend. My best friend gave it to me."

"But if you had to sell it. . . ."

"I would rather starve. I would indeed. I would rather die of hunger."

"It is certainly a beautiful piece."

"Yes, isn't it? But it is because my great friend gave it me that I value it. If she hadn't given it me I shouldn't value it so much."

"No. I daresay not. You lived in Exeter, didn't you, in your youth?"

"Yes." May Beringer sighed as though she were relieved at being in safety again. "I was very fond of Exeter."

"I wouldn't like to live in Exeter," said Agatha vigorously; "too sleepy."

"Oh, it wasn't sleepy in my time, I assure you," said May Beringer. "Not sleepy at all. No indeed. There was so much going on. All sorts of things were always happening."

"Really," said Agatha ironically, "I wouldn't have thought it. What kind of things?"

"Oh, I don't know," said May Beringer

vaguely. "Meeting one's friends and concerts, and in the summer we had picnics——"

"Picnics!" said Agatha scornfully.

"Yes, beautiful picnics they were too. We used to have the moors so close to us and on a fine day——"

She had a strange sense while they were talking all about nothing that she would fall asleep were she not careful. Her head was already nodding. It was because Agatha Payne's eyes were fixed upon her so persistently. The room went round and round. Then Agatha said something that woke her very sufficiently. "Do you know when you're going to die?"

May Beringer's eyes stared.

"To die? Oh no!"

"Do you want to know?"

"No, I don't. I don't want to think about it."

"Ah, you're a coward." Agatha was slipping the cards swiftly through her fingers, so that they were like live things.

"No, I'm not." May Beringer was close to tears. "But I don't want to think of it. It's not a thing you want to think of."

"Why not? It's coming some time. That's certain. It's better for many. Take yourself now. If your money gives out and you don't get a job, what are you going to do?"

"I don't want to think of it. Indeed I don't."

"But you ought to think of it. You ought to make provision. Who will you leave you things to?"

"My things?"

"Yes. Your odds and ends. That piece of amber, for instance."

"I hadn't thought of it." Poor May Beringer. All those forebodings that so resolutely she kept away from her were now crowding in.

"Haven't you made a will?" Agatha asked, rattling her cards like pistols.

"No. It didn't seem worth while."

"Well, I should make a will at once. You never know what will happen."

There was a little pause, then Agatha said again:

"You'd better know when you're going to die. Try the cards. They'll tell you."

"Oh no." May Beringer shrank back in her chair. "I shouldn't like that at all. I shouldn't approve of that. I don't think we're meant to know."

"Oh yes, we are." Agatha's black eyes never

left May Beringer's face. "Here, draw your chair up to the table. I'll show you."

"I'd really rather not, thank you. I have rather a headache. If you'll excuse me——"

"Nonsense. It will interest you. Come and have a look. You've never seen cards done the way I do them."

"I'd really rather not. . . ."

"Come along now."

In another moment May Beringer was sitting up, straight and stiff, beside the table. Opposite her, propped up against the wall, Miranda with unblinking eyes watched them.

Agatha Payne dealt out the cards. They lay in rows of six on the cloth.

"Nothing there," she said, swept them up, shuffled, and dealt again.

May Beringer stared with agonised intensity.

"There they are. Six of clubs. Queen of clubs, four of diamonds. Ah! This is you! Just as I thought. Eight of spades. . . ."

"Why am I the eight of spades?" May Beringer asked.

"It isn't you who are the eight of spades. It is the combination with the other cards. You're in danger——"

"In danger?" May echoed feebly.

"Yes. They show it quite distinctly. I'll deal some more. Four of hearts. Five of diamonds. Knave of clubs—yes, there you are— don't you see? Ten of spades—the ten with the knave of clubs and five of diamonds. You're threatened by something very serious indeed."

"Oh dear," said May Beringer, drawing back from the table as though she were afraid that she would contaminate herself by touching the cards. "This isn't right. Really it isn't. I think I'll go to bed if you don't mind."

Agatha put her hand on her arm. "Wait a minute. Let's see some more. We're just coming to the exciting part." She made a little pile of cards, a dozen on top of one another. Then she dealt another row of six.

"There you are," she said, as the eight of spades appeared. "Isn't it extraordinary? You're in luck to-night. They are coming out well. Now let's see."

She took a card—the king of clubs—from the pile, then another—the three of spades—yet another—the six of spades. "All black," she said, stroking her lip. "That settles it."

"Settles what?" asked May Beringer.

"According to the cards you have about a month to live. Of course there may be nothing in it. Still, it's an odd thing."

"It's wicked!" May Beringer cried, trembling all over as she rose from the table. "It's absolutely wicked. You should not do such things, Mrs. Payne! They aren't right. They are against religion."

Mrs. Payne grimly smiled. "I haven't much use for religion, if you ask me," she said. "You should make your will, you should indeed."

But May Beringer had, on occasion, courage. She pulled herself together, drew herself up, and said with great dignity:

"Good-night, Mrs. Payne—and thank you for a very pleasant evening."

But in her own room, when her door was closed, she caught Pip to her breast, and, holding him tightly, burst into a flood of agitated tears.

CHAPTER VII

DEATH OF HOPES

ON the 3rd of February, in the morning, Lucy Amorest's cousin died. She had made in January two attempts to see him, but had been no more successful than on her Christmas visit.

She had been, herself, needing all the courage that she could muster. She had not been very well. She had caught a cold in this wintry weather, and then there was the house. What exactly was the matter with the house she could not be sure, but six months ago it had been tolerable; now she disliked it so actively that soon she must leave it even, if needs must, for the highways and hedges. At the thought of the highways and hedges she smiled. She had an odd sense of humour, all her own, something detached and cynical and ironic. Ironic about herself. She would chuckle sometimes without a moment's notice in the middle of her undressing or lying awake at chilly morning hours or reading the

Standard, and the chuckle meant that she was seeing herself from the outside as something very ludicrous—ludicrous in its own importance about itself, in its little assumptions of dignity and eagerness and desire. When she saw herself in that way she lost all her anxieties and perturbations of spirit. So unimportant was she in the general scheme of things that it was absurd indeed to see how the little creature worried and fussed. Fuss and worry! worry and fuss! Every one at it, every one trying to get their money's worth, and the one thing that mattered—the love of God—scarcely entering their heads.

On such detached occasions she felt a human intimate relationship with Jesus Christ. That He had a sense of humour she well knew; if He had not, He would never be able to endure the eternal conceit and self-absorption of human beings. It was because He could laugh a little, seeing with His tenderness and understanding what children these humans were, that He could be so patient. She would never be so patient— and sometimes she was exasperated so keenly with herself that she could shake herself. During this month of January she felt just this half-ironical, half-kindly exasperation about herself. She *could* not put the thought of this money out of her head, and she *could* not feel a proper patience with May Beringer, and she *could* not have the kindly feelings that she ought to have towards old Agatha Payne.

Moreover, she had dreadful dark suspicions that she was a good deal of a snob. She didn't want to spend the rest of her days with women like May Beringer and Agatha Payne. She liked good talk and laughter and fun. No one enjoyed a really *silly* time more than she did. It was too bad that she must always have her laugh to herself. Never mind, when the money came she would go—— She pulled herself up. There she was again. Counting her chickens. She was ashamed of herself.

She caught her cold on her second visit to her cousin's house. It was a biting windy day, and once more the housekeeper talked to her in the doorway and refused to step aside. Horrible woman! Mrs. Amorest indulged in a nice, warm, consoling, comforting luxury of dislike on the way home. She could not abide the woman, and she was glad that she could not. She would like to give her a piece of her mind, and then she chuckled again because she was always such a failure at giving people pieces of her mind. She could never remain indignant for more than two minutes together. It never seemed worth while; she saw the ludicrous side of bad temper so quickly. Her husband used to say that it was very irritating of her. It was never worth while to lose one's temper with her.

She would never have heard of her cousin's death had it not been for her visit to the grocer's. Mrs. Conduit, the kind wife of the grocer, told her. He had died that morning in his sleep, and was to be buried on Thursday—service at St. John's—in the May Lane Cemetery.

The news threw her into a terrible agitation. She did not now think of the money, but only of the way that he had stroked her hair, falling asleep. Poor Cousin Francis. He had looked at her so kindly on that last visit. He had meant always to be kind, but it had been so wretched and gloomy for him in that large ugly house, always ill, always suffering. She shed tears in her room, sitting in front of the tiny fire thinking of him.

There was another thought waiting for her, but she kept it back. Her own loneliness. Her last relation was gone. She had no relations now and no friends in the whole world, save only her boy. The last of the family was gone. There were others perhaps somewhere, but she had long lost sight of them and they of her. The world was a large place to be alone in, but she prevented that thought from reaching her, keeping it behind her. Nevertheless, it was there with her in the room. She could not drive it out. She did not sleep at all that night, lying there during the hours that crept one by one to her bedside, nodded at her and stole off again. She read her Bible and her Prayer Book, but she could not bring them close to her. The house with its silent mutterings was all alive around her. Strange doors closed and opened, steps were on the stair, walls whispered. Her candle guttered, flamed upwards, died, and she had not another. Her room was very cold, and the dawn would never come. Mrs. Bloxam found her wide-eyed and shivering at eight o'clock.

Nevertheless, with the morning her spirit returned. Francis was happier now in Paradise, away from that unfriendly dwelling-place and his sufferings over. She liked to think of him in Paradise, his surprise at what he found there, his wide-eyed astonishment at the kindliness and the fun, the laughter and the flowers.

He would be young again, and instead of the grasping and acidulated Greenacre there would be St. Michael and all the angels. He would be no longer naked and alone. He would worry no more about his money, he would have finer things to think about. He would not be suspicious and imagine that people were making a fuss of him simply for what they could get out of him.

He would be learning, too, the beauties of service. He would be doing things for others. The angels would soon be setting him to jobs that would be new for him indeed. He would not like them at first. He would feel that he was wasting his time, and then, as happiness came flooding in, he would see that that was the only way *to* be happy. When he saw that, what a change it would make in him! He simply would not be the same man.

She amused herself with these thoughts, and saw it all so truly that any unhappiness she might have had about his fate left her—he was far better off than he had ever been.

The next thing was—what should she do about the funeral? Go, of course, although no card had been sent her; no word even of his death had yet come to her. She did not mind that. They were too busy to think of her. But—what should she wear? She had a black dress, but it was so shabby, so faded that it would never do. Her grey silk was all that she had, and that would seem too gay at a funeral. But there was a black silk scarf given her many years ago by a friend. And her bonnet of dark purple. And her black gloves.

She would like to send some flowers, but the thought that this might seem ostentatious and pushing restrained her. She bought on the Thursday morning a bunch of early snowdrops, and thought that she would have an opportunity of putting them on the grave.

Thursday was a lovely day, one of those February days that come in Glebeshire and seem to promise an immediate bountiful spring. The sky was clear-washed to a blue that was almost white; clouds, fragments of faintest lawn, floated so lightly that they seemed to be blown, as in a children's game, from place to place. The woods that fringed the hills were shadowed the most delicate rose, and behind the shadows were softly dark, like velvet. The air was clear and still, so that the shouts of children and the barking of dogs and the rattle of wheels could be distinctly heard.

She found the walk up to St. John's a climb. This was a dark stuffy church with heavy green windows, stony-faced cherubs, and a shining cold floor. She slipped in at the back, unnoticed. She was surprised at the number of people present. She had thought of him always as a lonely man with no friends, but the church was quite full. There was a subdued murmur of voices and much moving of heads to see who was who.

At first she knew no one, and then she saw Mr. Neilson, her banker, and then Mr. Agnew, the kind little solicitor, with his bald shiny head and broad resolute back. In spite of herself, at the sight of him, her heart beat. He, in all probability, knew the contents of Cousin Francis's will, and he seemed to her for the moment to be the arbiter of all the fates and destinies of the world.

Then she saw Miss Greenacre, darkened with a thick black veil, come slowly up the aisle. The coffin was in front of the altar covered with flowers. The organ began to play and the choir filed in. The sun seemed to blow in gusts

through the green windows and to run in patterns
up and down the floor. It was very cold, and
smelt as though the church were always closed.

She could not attend to the service. Her confidence about Cousin Francis's happiness was
gone. It was so lonely for him. She could not
drive from her consciousness the feeling that it
was he who was there in that coffin. She knew,
of course, that it was not so. It was only the
worthless clay; but the chilliness and the green
light and all the casual black heads of the indif-
ferent people depressed her so that soon she was
crying between the fingers of her worn black
gloves. A stout man next her pushed and heaved
as though he were wishing for release, and the
organ went on wailing like a peevish child.

Outside, when they started to walk to the
cemetery, it was better. Although they moved
slowly they were soon in the lanes above Orange
Street, and here it was very beautiful. The trees
were bare, but you could feel their happiness at
the consciousness of the strong sap that was pouring through their veins. The sky was as clear as
egg-shell china, and once and again there was a
break in the hedge showing fields as fresh as
watered silk. How incongruous that black, slow,

silent procession! The carriages crawled re-
luctantly; in subdued voices the mourners spoke.
Lucy Amorest walked nearly at the last. No one
had addressed a word to her that day.

When they turned into the cemetery they were
on the hillside, and all the valley of the Pol lay
below them. On the side of the hill opposite
to them was the grim stone house, a speck in
the distance, that had been Cousin Francis's
home. It looked so unimportant now beside the
gay shining beauty of the town that sprawled on
the hillside, and over all the Cathedral sailed,
in the clear light, away, away, away, so lightly
set that it seemed that another tug of the wind
would release it and send it flying to heaven.

They crowded about the open grave. The
clergyman, thin and peaked, his surplice blowing
in the breeze, said the last words. The coffin
was lowered. Words were indistinct, and human
beings unimportant. Mrs. Amorest could not
see the grave; she caught fragments of the white
surplice, and, clutching in her glove the snowdrops, felt that she had not courage to step forward and throw them down on to the coffin. No
one regarded her. She was as though she had
never existed. They did not know that he had

stroked her hair and said that she was better than all the others. Well, it did not matter. He knew and she knew. He was aware now that she had tried to see him and had been prevented. There was now an understanding between them as there had never been when he was alive. Miss Green-acre was of no further importance; she could not come between them any more.

She walked back very slowly as the afternoon light gathered in, but she was not unhappy. She was very glad that she had been able to go, and she gave the snowdrops to a little street child who stared at her with wide-open eyes, too deeply astonished to thank her.

Four days later she received this letter from the little bald-headed solicitor:

DEAR MRS. AMOREST—I wonder whether you will be passing one morning and could look in and see me for a moment. I have something that I should like to dis-cuss with you if you have time to give me.—I beg to remain, yours sincerely,

JOHN H. AGNEW.

Time to give him! The letter shook in her hand. Time to give him! The crisis of all her life had come. The breakfast things on the table were dim, the rose-coloured furniture, the shad-owed, misty air. Only, through the haze, looking up, she saw distinctly Agatha Payne in the doorway staring at her.

It was so obvious that important news had come to her that she did not attempt to disguise it. But faintly behind her agitation she felt an anger that had been piling up in her breast for days at the way that Agatha Payne had now of coming into her room uninvited and unheralded. Whether the woman made a pretence of knocking or no she could not tell, but look up and there she would be in her old dirty purple gown leaning against the wall. She had apparently now a great purpose of showing herself friendly, but active friendliness did not come easily from her. What was the old woman about? This morning she was direct enough. She said at once, coming to the table and pointing with her thick, shapeless finger:

"You've had a letter about the money?"

Then, as Mrs. Amorest said nothing, she went on in her thick, guttural voice, "I know he died nearly a week ago. You went to the funeral. So you needn't try to hide it from me."

"Hide it from you," Lucy Amorest said, looking up. "I wasn't trying to do that. Why should I?"

Indeed her excitement was so great that she did not, at the moment, mind Agatha Payne knowing anything she pleased. Nevertheless she would not have her coming into the room like that without so much as a knock.

"Would you mind, dear," she said, smiling, but speaking with firmness, "knocking before you come in? It is pleasanter, don't you think, for both of us?"

But Agatha Payne had not heard. She had one hand pressed to her bosom and with the other she was still pointing.

"What does he say in the letter? Does he say that you've got the money?"

"He says I'm to go and see him," Mrs. Amorest answered. "It may not be about the money at all."

"Of course it is. What else should he want to see you about? Aren't you in luck? Well, I never! Whatever will you do with it all?"

Then, after a little pause, she added, "When are you going to see him?"

"I shall go this morning, I think. I may as well."

"I should think you'd better. I couldn't wait a minute if it was me." She stared at Mrs.

Amorest as though she would devour her. She slowly sucked her fingers, one after another. Then she withdrew to the door.

"I shall like to know," she said, "what he says to you."

"Oh, I daresay," answered Mrs. Amorest brightly, "that it won't be anything at all."

But in her heart she knew that, were that so, she would suffer great disappointment. Her knees trembled as she felt her way down the dark old stairs of the house. Her heart thumped as though it would hammer her body to pieces. All the scene was dark before her.

Mr. Agnew the solicitor lived in Hampden Street near the Market-place and to the left of Orange Street. It was a dark, poky little street, but it debouched on to a twist of the Pol which, in the unexpected way that it had, sauntered into the city and then hurried out to the hills and fields again. Mr. Agnew's number was nine, and his office was on the third floor. At the bottom of the stairs she rested. Did her heart not beat less wildly she thought that she would never reach the top. It was amazing that ordinary life should push so tumultuously around her. A boy passed the door, whistling. A man with a cart cried out that he had vegetables to sell. The Cathedral bells began to ring. A donkey hee-hawed, a child cried, and the sun flickered in pools about the stairs. All this as though nothing tremendous were happening to her at all. She laughed at herself then and the laugh helped her forward. How absurd of her to imagine that her affairs mattered to anybody! After all these years even that simple lesson was not yet learnt.

She climbed the stairs and knocked on the door that had "Agnew & Pace, Solicitors," upon its glass.

"Come in," said some one.

She went in, and a young boy wearing a bright blue tie, a large horseshoe pin, and a very confident air asked her what she wanted.

"Mr. Agnew wrote to me," she said timidly, "and asked me to come and see him."

"Would you mind giving me your name, ma'am?" said the bright young man.

"Mrs. Amorest is my name."

"I'll tell Mr. Agnew. He's engaged at the moment. Would you take a seat, please?"

Mrs. Amorest sat down, but it was terribly hard to wait. To be so near and yet to be kept without information. The room was so cold and so hard, with a map of England on one shining wall and a photograph of Polchester Cathedral on the other, and the young man working so earnestly at the table. All so quiet that the clock on the mantelpiece seemed the only live thing there.

At last the bell rang, and the young man said very politely, "Will you go in now, ma'am, if you please?"

For a horrible moment she was afraid lest her knees should refuse to support her. She did tremble for an instant when she stood, then bravely she moved forward. She was reassured when she saw the kindly smiling face of Mr. Agnew. He surely could have nothing but good news for her when he smiled at her like that. He came forward to meet her, shook her by the hand, set out a chair for her. He was a short stumpy man with a broad back. His broad back and round, shining bald head were the two features that, on every occasion, freshly astonished Mrs. Amorest.

"Well, that is good of you," he said in his warm friendly voice—but his words were always a little measured, as though he had to pay for each one and was determined not to be extravagant. "I do hope that it has been no trouble for you to come in and see me?"

"No trouble, thank you," said Mrs. Amorest, trembling in spite of herself.

"Really, the weather is very pleasant," he went on, rubbing his hands cheerfully together, "Very pleasant, indeed."

"Yes," said Mrs. Amorest, smiling faintly.

"And one's always taken in afresh," he went on. "That's the curious thing. Always believes spring's arriving, although of course it can't be so early in the year. And then back the frost comes and all the buds are nipped and the flowers ruined."

"Yes. It is strange," Mrs. Amorest admitted.

"What I say is," went on Mr. Agnew, smiling broadly and showing two splendid rows of white teeth, "that the climate's changing. To my mind there can be no doubt of it—no doubt at all. Permanently, I mean. They say it's the icebergs —and I shouldn't wonder. Tricky things, icebergs. Ever been to America, Mrs. Amorest?"

"No, never."

"Well, I remember a voyage I took over there to see about some client's affairs—when was it?

Let me see, in '82, I think—or was it '83? Never mind. . . . Whenever it was, we got into the thick of those beastly things. Pretty they were. Green like glass. But dangerous! My word! The Captain didn't have his clothes off for three days and nights. Lucky we were to come through as we did."

"You must have been alarmed," said Mrs. Amorest.

"Yes, we were. Icebergs and fogs. Those are the things you have to look out for at sea. All the same we had a good Captain. That's the principal thing. Queer place, America. Well, well . . ."

He stood there smiling, rubbing his hands together, and Mrs. Amorest sat in her chair, also smiling and rubbing *her* hands together. In spite of herself she felt faint. She could not see the room clearly and she was very cold.

"I do really hope it's been no trouble to you coming to see me."

"Oh, none at all, Mr. Agnew."

"Well, that's good. That's fine. Let me see —where were we? Oh yes! Quite so. Quite so."

He stood over his table fingering papers. He

picked them up and put them down. "Oh yes!"
He drew himself up and looked towards her.
"What I asked you to come and see me about,
Mrs. Amorest, was just this. Your cousin Francis
Bulling's death was very sad. Very sad, indeed.
But he'd been ailing for a long time. You were
not at the funeral, I think?"

"I was there."

"Oh, you were! Indeed! I call that wonderful of you, such a climb as it is up to that cemetery. A terrible business for catching a cold, a
funeral, especially in the winter-time. I would
hardly have expected you to be present. I always
say that one funeral means a dozen." He looked
up, smiling broadly. "But I'm glad you're none
the worse. I am, indeed."

She waited, her hands folded on her lap.

"Where were we? Oh yes, it was about his
will that I asked you to drop in. The fact is
that he's left you something expressly by name."

"That was very good of him," said Mrs.
Amorest.

"Yes, he was a good-natured man, Francis
Bulling, at heart. He didn't like to show his
feelings. That's a British trait to hide our feelings. Most of us are the same that way and I

must say I think it's a pity. Many of us are not given credit for the feelings we have got. Now the French are supposed to be all feeling, but I assure you that at heart I'd back an Englishman every time. Very superficial, the French."

"Yes," said Mrs. Amorest.

Now to come to the point. I'll read you what he says—'To my cousin, Lucy Amorest, I would wish to leave some personal possession of mine that she may choose, that she may keep it and remember me by it.' There you are. That's exactly what the will says. He's done the same to several others, his housekeeper Miss Greenacre and one or two more. It shows that he had more feeling than appeared at first sight."

Mrs. Amorest said nothing.

"The executors selected a few things, and to save you trouble I have one or two here in the office. If none of them struck you as very inviting, then you might like to go up to the house and choose something there. But they seemed to me very serviceable—very serviceable, indeed. There's an especially fine ink-pot and . . . but you shall see for yourself."

He rang his bell. The smart boy appeared in the doorway.

"Just bring in those things of Mr. Bulling's, Charlie. They are in that farther cupboard. Carefully now. Carefully. We don't want anything broken."

Charlie reappeared, his arms loaded. He placed the things, very reverently, on the table in front of Mr. Agnew. There was a large and very heavy inkstand, a blue leather writing-case, an ivory paper-knife with a silver handle, a small silver match-box, and a glass paper-weight stamped with red and blue flowers.

"Now, Mrs. Amorest," said Mr. Agnew cheerfully, "here they are. And do tell us quite honestly if none of these strike your fancy. There are plenty of other things up at the house, but I thought we might save you the trouble of a journey. The point after all is to have something to remember him by—something you'll have on the table in front of you."

"I think," said Mrs. Amorest quietly, "I should like the match-box."

"Would you, indeed?" said Mr. Agnew heartily. "Well, I must say that seems to me a very wise choice. I agree with you. It's small

—takes up very little room, and it's altogether a handsome affair. Francis Bulling used it himself thousands of times, I've no doubt at all." He rang the bell again.

"Charlie, just wrap this up in paper for Mrs. Amorest, will you? She'll take it along with her."

There was silence while Charlie wrapped up the match-box. Mrs. Amorest said nothing, but sat there, without moving, her hands folded. Mr. Agnew was uncomfortable. He did not know why. He, who was never at a loss, had nothing to say. He had expected that the old lady would be pleased that her cousin should have remembered her. But she was always quiet; never showed what she was feeling. Nice old lady. One of the old kind that were getting rarer. Like the climate, people were changing. Every one levelling up. He couldn't say that he liked it. Much harder to get good clerks now than it used to be. Ah, there was Charlie with the parcel.

"That's right. That's right. Sure you've got everything? Mind you come in and see me if there's ever anything I can do for you. Only too delighted. Good-day. That's the door. Then down three flights. Do hope it hasn't tired you."

After she was gone he stood at his window looking out upon the sun-dappled Pol, the shining field, the houses with their red-brown flanks rejoicing in the unexpected warmth. She was old. Hard on one to be as alone in the world as that at her age. Nice old lady, too. He felt the bulging muscle of his arm, smiled, and went to his work.

CHAPTER VIII

MAY BERINGER TRIES TO ESCAPE

DEEP down in her cellar Agatha Payne was working. She was working with an energy, an enthusiasm, a fidelity to her new ambition that she had not known for years. She had now a purpose. She saw, glittering through the thick and misted cellar light, the sheen and splendour of the most beautiful treasure of the world—*her* treasure, her gold and ruby amber, hers, always hers, stolen from her by that long, thin, ridiculous old maid whom she could frighten by a whisper, terrify with a chuckle.

She liked so to terrify. It gave her hot and sensuous pleasure when she saw the cheeks of that foolish old woman blanch; her heart beat thick when she saw tears tremble on those red-rimmed weak eyelids. Ah! she would make them fall before she had done!

And so her two pleasures went arm in arm together! She could lead them both by the hand—her lust for power and her lust for that piece of liquid ruby, that stout-set, bold, and scornful dragon standing so firmly on his amber pedestal.

She was awake as she had not been for years. All her energies were active. No more lazy lying in her old chair tossing her scarlet slipper in the air, no more crumbling of nougat out of its paper packet, no more half-dreamy watching the silver-finned fish as they sailed with gaping jaws about the room. She had work to do, and work that must not wait.

The first thing that must be ascertained was the time when old Lucy Amorest would receive her money. Everything depended on that. Once the old fool was in command of it, very little further effort would be needed. She would ask for a loan of twenty, thirty, fifty, a hundred pounds. The old thing would not refuse it; she was a foolish old woman always wanting to give something away.

There was a trouble, then, that that long stick of a Beringer would not wish to sell. A present from a friend, she had said—her dearest friend. She could soon be frightened into changing her mind. The time would come when she would promise anything in order to be free. To be free of what? Of terror and dismay. That she and her wretched dog might go to sleep at nights without a sudden waking. There was only a thin wall between the one room and the other. So much could be done with a thin wall at midnight!

But she did not, as yet, plan anything very terrible. Only a little fun, entering into it with something of the spirit with which one boy bullies another, even with a sort of good humour. But she must have the red amber. It was hers, had been hers long before the Beringer woman had seen it. Centuries ago her fingers had closed around its firm cold sides, felt its beating strength, watched the light slip and coil and unfurl about its heart. It had been hers since the beginning of time and It knew it.

Her impatience on the morning after Mrs. Amorest's visit to her solicitor was urgent. She could not keep quiet, but was dressed before Mrs. Bloxam came in with her breakfast.

"Poor Mrs. Hamorest!" said Mrs. Bloxam. "She's 'ad a bad night. Couldn't sleep a wink, she tells me." Then she looked at Mrs. Payne with mild surprise: "You're up early, ma'am."

Although she was not naturally very sharp, her interest in the old ladies quickened her observation, and afterwards, when events forced her to look back, she recorded to interested friends her distinct impression that "things had been going on. She looked different, all sharp like, and as though she was listenin' for something. She was a queer one, that old Mrs. Payne. Not quite right in 'er 'ead, a long way back, if you ask me."

Mrs. Payne indeed was very sharp this morning, and it was not long before she was fumbling with the handle of Mrs. Amorest's door. On entering, she suffered quite a shock of surprise at that old lady's appearance. She was not given to thinking of others, especially when, as now, she was herself driven by one dominating desire, but even her almost crazy egotism was pierced by the forlorn, sick appearance that Mrs. Amorest presented.

She had not been expecting a visitor, and she sat listlessly at her table, her hands in front of her, her eyes fixed on some distant point.

She had always, when Mrs. Payne had seen her, presented a brave front to the world, and something deeply hidden in Mrs Payne's better part had subconsciously admired that. She was not, however, now moved to any kindness or pity. Her only thought was of the money.

"Good morning," she said huskily.

Mrs. Amorest looked up, and, seeing her, passed her hand over her eyes as though she would drive from them some unwanted vision.

"Good morning, Agatha," she said gently.

"I came in," Agatha said huskily, moving towards the table, "to ask you about the money. Is it all right?"

"The money?"

"Yes—the money your cousin left you."

"I was wrong about that. He hasn't left me any money."

"He hasn't——?"

"No. He didn't do what he said he would. I was silly to believe in it."

"He's left you nothing?"

"Something of his to remember him by. I chose a little thing of his—his match-box."

"And that's all?"

"Yes. Why should he? I was only his cousin. It was very kind of him to think of me."

"Then he cheated you."

"Oh, no. I cheated myself. It was only one

day he was feeling kindly. I happened to be there. He would have said it to any one else who was kind to him."

"I say he cheated you." Agatha Payne's voice was hoarse with anger. "He said he'd give it to you. He made a solemn promise. May he rot in hell, I say."

Mrs. Amorest was frightened. She had known for a long time that the woman was queer, but there was something about that tall, fat, shapeless figure standing now right over her, something in those staring black eyes and that deep reverberating voice that filled her with a new alarm. The woman was mad. Mrs. Amorest wanted to be alone. What had any one else to do with her affairs? She must think things out. She was face to face with the sharpest crisis of her life. But it was her crisis. No one else had anything to do with it. Why should it be of importance to Agatha Payne whether she had her money or no? She felt, too, in the last fierce words that the woman had used, some sudden obtrusion from another world of experience that had not been, and never could be, her own. She had called her Agatha and had been called by her Lucy, but she had been always aware that there could be no real contact between them. And now she seemed to see, in a flash of revelation, that Agatha Payne's past had been worlds away from her most esoteric imagination. There were twists of a life that was as strange to her as the manners and customs of the natives of Central Africa.

"It's kind of you to be interested, Agatha," she said; "but there's nothing more to be said about it. It was only an idea that I had that he might leave me something. I shouldn't have spoken to you about it."

"No, you should not." The other woman turned savagely upon her. "Making me believe things that were not true. It's wicked—a wicked shame. And you'll pay for it. No one's deceived me yet and not paid for it. You just wait."

She threw up her head as though she would spit upon her, then half-lurched, half-stumbled from the room. Back in her own place she cursed and swore like the old gipsy that she was. That mild, milk-faced old woman had taken her in, pretending this and pretending that. Just to make herself more important. She had always known that no money was coming to her. Talked like that to amuse herself. Amuse herself! She'd amuse her before she was finished with her! Her knees were trembling and she flopped into her chair. The fish came out of the tank and swam, circling about her head. Miranda, like some familiar spirit, sat and watched her, her beady eyes fixed in some sort of grim satisfaction upon her plight. The sharp pain constricted about her head, binding it ever and ever more tightly. Then, slowly, it withdrew. Thoughts moved clearly and steadily once more through the air that was now cooler and the light that was now stronger. Mrs. Amorest faded into dim background. But more powerfully than ever before the piece of red amber shone before her eyes. What is this lust of possession, this ache and longing for the absolute power of dominion? Napoleon moving towards Moscow, Philip II. stretching his fingers over the Netherlands, the vineyard of Naboth, Marie Antoinette and her fatal necklace, Piemente and the box of moidores, Agatha Payne and her piece of red amber—the soul alone knoweth its secret tyrannies.

She sat there all day until evening.

She sprawled back in her chair and saw it gleaming there on her mantelpiece in front of her. Surely it was there! She knew now its

every shade and glitter and trembling light.
Well, if there was to be no money there was the
other way. The Beringer woman should give it
to her whether she wanted or no—yes, if she
must wring that scraggy old neck to get it.

She got up at last and made herself some
cocoa, then moved out towards May Beringer's
room.

She stayed outside the door and gave two
knocks, one loud and abrupt, the other soft, an
echo of the first. While she stood there a smile
was on her lips. That will make her jump. *That*
will make her jump. She's frightened now. She
knows it's me. And her dog is frightened. He
knows too. He's under the bed. On her side of
the door she fancied that she could hear the other
woman's frightened breathing, sharp and hurried. She's standing there with her head on one
side, waiting. She hopes I'll go away. She's
praying that I will.

Then she knocked again, loudly.

"Come in," said the whisper of a voice.

She pushed open the door and went in with
jollity, laughing. "Well, Miss Beringer, and
how are you finding yourself? I thought I'd
pay you a little call. I've just drunk my cup of

cocoa, and half an hour's talk with you before going to bed will do me good."

She moved across the room as though she owned it, and pulling out the roomiest chair plumped down in it. She sat in her accustomed attitude, one knee over the other. Her eyes were fixed on the red amber that now was in shadow and glowed a smouldering ruby. That was the pedestal; the dragon stood translucent gold.

May Beringer, untidy, confused, stood like an owl bewildered by unexpected light. Her hand was at her thin bony breast.

"I'm not so well, thank you," she said. She looked indeed to-day infinitely old and worn. "I haven't been sleeping too well." She broke then, with a kind of hurried speech as though she had but little time, into a most eager appeal. "Mrs. Payne, tell me—why are you persecuting me like this? Why do you come to my room? Why did you knock on my wall last night? I haven't done anything to harm you. I haven't hurt you in any way. I never saw you before I came here. I never interfered with you. I know it's silly of me to go on like this, but I haven't been sleeping——" she broke off. She had been struggling with her tears. They came now trickling through her hands that she pressed to her face. She collapsed on to a chair and sat there, her head forward.

Mrs. Payne said nothing. The dog appeared from under the bed. After hesitating a moment he came forward slowly and pressed himself, all huddled up, against his mistress's foot. She looked up and went on slowly, jabbing a rather dirty handkerchief against her nose:

"I know it's silly of me to go on like this. It's foolish of me and weak, I know. But I'm really not well. If I don't get my sleep my health always suffers. You must excuse me. I'm not so young as I used to be. I've been feeling much older this winter. But won't you leave me alone? I've done you no harm."

Agatha Payne was savouring an exquisite and delicious pleasure as she watched her. It was not a pleasure of cruelty nor of passion, but rather of power, and also of a deep consciousness of sensation. She almost liked May Beringer as she sat there snivelling; a very little more, and she could have gone and put her arms around her and comforted her. But she had not known many sensations in the last year or two—only her cards and her food and her cup of cocoa.

She was happy now as she had not been for many a day.

At last she spoke in her strange bass voice, deep like a man's.

"You are imagining things," she said. "You are ill. The cards said you were going to be."

"That's it," May Beringer broke out. "Why did you show them to me? What made you? I know I'm silly if you put things into my head. I always was as a girl. I've been like that ever since I was a child. I'm not going to die I'm not going to die. I'm not going to die!"

Her voice was almost a scream.

"The cards said so," Agatha Payne answered slowly. "I didn't make them come as they did."

Miss Beringer turned and looked at the other woman with a considering gaze as though she were seeing her for the first time. "Why do you hate me? I've never done you any harm. You came here. I didn't ask you to come."

"I came because I wanted to be kind to you, because I thought you were lonely."

"I'm not lonely," May Beringer broke out desperately. "I'm not at all. I don't want anybody. I can get on by myself."

"I like you," said Agatha Payne, smiling. "I like to be with you. I enjoy our little talks. Perhaps I'm the lonely one."

"No, you're not," said May Beringer excitedly. "You're not lonely at all. But you want to tease me and frighten me. And you want something else. You want my piece of amber."

Mrs. Payne said nothing.

"That's what you want. You can't deny it. But you won't have it, however much you want it. I'll put the police after you if you take it. I'll have you put in prison. Yes, I will. I'll have you put in prison.

She was in a state of terrible excitement.

"Who says that I want it?" said Agatha Payne quietly. "You have strange ideas in your head. You are ill. You should see a doctor."

May Beringer made a great effort at control. She sat, staring in front of her, as though she were summoning all her forces to her aid. At last more quietly she said:

"Yes, I am ill—at least not well. My back is very painful." Then she added with real dignity: "I think we can't be friends. We are too unlike one another. I am an old woman now, and it's too late to change myself. And I'm easily frightened. Perhaps at nothing. I don't know. But I do ask you not to come and visit me any more."

"When you're ill," said Mrs. Payne, "in bed and can't move, you'll want somebody. You'll be glad to see me, perhaps."

"I'm not going to be ill. Do you hear? I'm not going to be ill. I know you want me to be ill. You're wishing me to be ill now. But I won't be ill. You want me to die, and then you can have the piece of amber; but I'm not going to die. It's only my back. That will be better to-morrow, and I'm going to sleep even though you do knock on the wall."

"Knock on the wall!" repeated Agatha Payne scornfully. "Who says I knock on the wall?"

"You do! You know you do!" May Beringer cried, rising to her feet. She pointed to the door. "I don't want you in here. You are not to come again. It's my room. I can have whom I like. I forbid you to come any more."

Agatha Payne nodded her head. "I shall come when I like," she said. "You can't stop me." Then she added slowly: "But if you'll give me that piece of amber I won't come any more."

May Beringer snatched it from the mantelpiece

as though she feared that it would vanish from before her face. "Nobody shall have it," she said. "It's the only thing I've got."

Agatha Payne rose slowly and went to the door. "We'll see," she said. "We'll see."

There was no knocking on the wall that night, and May Beringer fell into a strange, heavy, confused sleep in which dreams were for ever forming a tapestry of illusion near her, showing her their sombre and kindling colour but always distant and indistinct. The piece of amber was there, and Jane Betts and Pip, and behind these a dark lowering sense of danger.

She did not wake when Mrs. Bloxam brought her her tea, and it was midday when that kind woman finally roused her with a shake on the shoulder, telling her that the sun was shining and that she had brought her a fresh cup, not wishing to disturb her earlier, she seemed so "proper drowsy."

She awoke with a great start, sitting up in bed with a consciousness that something terrible had happened to her. What was it? Ah, of course she knew. She must escape from here. Dreadful danger was hanging over her head. She must be away. . . . But how? when? where? While

Mrs. Bloxam was scattering about the room, making things a little brighter and more comfortable, she was endeavouring to compose her brain. She sat up in bed, her hands to her head. Her brain worked so slowly now. She could not see clearly. Things would not hang together. But one fact was plain. She must leave this house, and at once. She could not be another night under the same roof with that terrible wicked woman. And she must escape secretly. No one must know. Otherwise that woman would find out where she had gone and would follow her. She must return to St. Lennan, the place that she ought never to have left, to her old friend with whom she had lodged for so long. She would find work there. There must be something that she could do, even though it were only to sweep the floor. Were her back not so painful there were many things that she could do. She seemed filled with energy under the impulse of her terror. If only she might escape from this house never to see its walls again! She was now in a fever of agitation. She seemed to be in a moment practical and far-seeing. When did the trains go to St. Lennan? The day was moving on. The afternoons at this time of the year were very short. She must be away before dusk. She was out of bed and moving rapidly about the room, a strange figure, with her long sloping body, her loosened grey hair, moving restlessly from spot to spot in her grey flannel nightdress and her old bedroom slippers.

"Why, miss, whatever is the matter?" Mrs. Bloxam asked, realising her agitation.

"Mrs. Bloxam," Miss Beringer said, catching the other's stout arm, "have you got such a thing as a time-table about you?"

"About me, miss?" said Mrs. Bloxam, slapping her dirty apron. "No, miss, I can't say as I 'ave."

"Do you think you could get one for me?"

"A time-table, miss?" Mrs. Bloxam was all eyes. "Why, you'll catch your death o' cold wandering about like that, miss. 'Ere, let me get you your woolly waistcoat. A time-table? Well, I'm sure I don't know. A local, miss?"

"Yes. A Glebeshire one."

"Well, I'm sure I don't know. Mrs. Carstairs next door might 'ave one."

"Do go and see. Won't you? Please. Do go and see whether you can get one. A Glebeshire one. All the trains in Glebeshire. It's so important. At once. Now. Please. Please."

"At once, miss? And your fire ain't lit and you 'aven't drunk a drop of your tea."

"Oh, never mind about that. Please don't bother about that. If you'd only go at once."

"Well, I'm sure. Why? Are you going away, miss?"

"Yes, I am. I must. I'm not well here. I must go away at once. And, Mrs. Bloxam, I'll pay you your wages up to the end of the week. I'm so sorry to leave you. You've been so kind to me. But I have to go away—at once. Without losing a minute."

"Well, miss, I'm sure—— It don't matter about the bit of wages, but going out on an afternoon like this and you as delicate as you are—I shouldn't like——"

"It's all right. It is, really. It's perfectly all right. I'm going to friends."

"But whatever will you do about your things? You can't take them all with you sudden-like."

"I'll send for them. I'll give you an address to send them to. But please, please get me a time-table. And don't say a word to anybody.

Not a word. I do beg you not to say a word to anybody."

Miss Beringer had been pouring all this forth in an agitated whisper, looking at every instant towards the door as though expecting it to open and reveal the hated figure.

Mrs. Bloxam patted her on the shoulder. "There, there. Don't you worry. I'll get you the time-table."

After she was gone May Beringer dressed, pulling on her clothes as though she had but a moment to escape, and talking, as was her habit, in the same agitated whisper to Pip, who followed her every movement with nervous, anxious eyes.

"We mustn't stay, Pip. We mustn't, indeed. She'll do us some harm if we do. She'll do us both harm. You know you're as afraid of her as I am. She hates us both, Pip, and she wants to steal our things. She's a bad woman, Pip. She'd be a thief if she could. She's a bad, wicked woman. But she's not going to get what she wants. We'll get out of her way and go back to our friends, who'll be so glad to see us, and you'll be able to have exercise as you ought to and run on the sands again. You'll like that, won't you, Pip—and we won't be frightened any more. If only my back didn't hurt, Pip, we could have such a good time. Perhaps it will be better when we are beside the sea again. The sea air always did us good, didn't it, Pip?"

When Mrs. Bloxam returned, May Beringer was wearing her hat and was quite ready to go out.

"Have you got it, Mrs. Bloxam?" she asked in a whisper.

"Yes, miss, I've got it. It's an old one. Last November. But I daresay the trains are the same."

"I expect they are." She clutched at the little green flimsy time-table and began eagerly to turn the pages.

"Here we are." She read down the page. "Yes, there's a train at 3.30. There are very few trains. I mustn't miss that one. It seems to be the last. Three-thirty, and it's now quarter past two. That will do very nicely."

"What will you be doing about your bag, miss? You can't carry it all that way by yourself."

"Oh no, Mrs. Bloxam. I shall only take this small bag, and I'll catch the omnibus at the corner of Malpas Street. That will be quite easy. And now, Mrs. Bloxam, I do beg of you not to say a word to anybody—in any case not to-day. Will you promise me that?"

"Yes, miss, I promise."

"And I'll write to you from where I'm going, so that you can send the other things on. And here's your money."

She opened her old faded green purse and counted out the money. Then followed a very touching little scene, Mrs. Bloxam begging her to keep it until she could afford to pay her, or at least until the end of her journey, but May Beringer was firm. Mrs. Bloxam must be paid. They then shook hands.

"I'm sure, miss, I wish you every kind of good fortune," Mrs. Bloxam said.

"Thank you, Mrs. Bloxam, you've been a very kind friend."

Left alone she paused and listened, her hard ugly black straw hat a little askew on her head, Pip's chain in her hand. There was no sound. No one was moving through the house. The woman had left her alone for that time at least.

She had pushed things into her shabby black handbag helter-skelter, then feverishly pressed its

gaping lips together and insisted on their closing.
With the same excitement she affixed the chain
to Pip's collar while he stood by, little shivers of
excitement shuddering along his body. Then
very softly she opened the door, peered out, saw
nobody, and on tiptoe started down the stairs.

Arrived in the square, the sun round and
orange above the crooked roofs, she looked for a
moment back at the house, grim and grey above
her, the windows blind-eyed in its ancient corpse-
like body. Oh! might she never see it again! That
was her prayer. Never, never! She would like to
have said good-bye to Mrs. Amorest, who had been
kind to her, but she would write to her from St.
Lennan when, safe and secure, she could snap
her fingers at her recent terrors. She heard the
Cathedral clock ringing out the hour, and in a
panic scurried down the square dragging Pip
after her. The bag was heavy; her back seemed
to have a red-hot needle thrust through its spine,
but the thought of her escape heartened her to
the forgetting of all ills. She stood at the corner
of Malpas Street breathing heavily, waiting for
the omnibus. A new alarm beset her. Perhaps
they did not allow dogs in omnibuses? Whatever then should she do? She had not money

for a cab. There would not be time to walk. Tears filled her eyes, and, as though he realised that he was the cause of the trouble, Pip gazed up at her with beseeching gaze.

The omnibus came lolloping up, and she was glad to see that there were but two passengers inside it, and the conductor was a fresh-faced, kindly-looking young man.

"Oh, I do hope you don't mind a dog," she panted at him. "It's only as far as the station."

"Well, it's not strictly allowed," he said, trying to look severely at her, but pulling the string to send the omnibus farther in its journey; "but it's for the other passengers to say. If they object——"

"I do hope that you don't object," said Miss Beringer, jerked down on to her seat (they were now crossing the cobbles of the Market-place); "I am only going as far as the station, and he's a very well-behaved little dog. You can see how well-behaved he is."

The two passengers were a stout man with a red face, who simply nodded his head in a dignified manner but said nothing, and a young woman with a face like an apple and a hearty smile. She said that she liked dogs, and that her husband had several, and that he was a dear little fellow, and he reminded her of a dog that her father had had once who had also been a dear little fellow and had been run over by a butcher's cart, which was the worst of keeping pets because something dreadful always happened to them, watch them as you might.

The friendliness of the omnibus cheered Miss Beringer considerably, and with every jerk she was taking a farther step from the enemy. It was the hour before the winter dusk, and all the town was bathed in a yellow opalescent shadow. Houses and doors and windows were transfigured. As the omnibus climbed the hill to the station, the hills and fields beyond Seatown came into view, swimming in golden air. The river flashed like a bar of music heard unexpectedly. The houses darkened even as they passed them.

"We're a long way over the shortest day," said the amiable young woman, "but it doesn't seem to make much difference."

Up on the hill where the station was, there was a blowing hearty air. The station platform was exposed, and you could see from it low levels of green fields, a wood now purple dark, and a cottage silver in the early dusk. There was no one about. She sank down on to the hard platform seat, gathering Pip into her skirt. Every bone in her body was aching, and she seemed to have so many bones—more than the average number, she was sure. She would not buy her ticket for a moment; there was plenty of time. She liked to look across to the quiet fields and the masts of trees black and silver against the orange sky. So peaceful and so quiet after the last days and nights. It was past three o'clock, but there was plenty of time. There was no movement about the station.

A train against a side platform whistled and jolted away. A porter passed, looked at her for a moment and then walked on.

She sat in a sort of blissful dream. The thought of returning to St. Lennan was wonderful to her. Indeed, she should never have left it. The fear that she might not be able to earn her living seemed to disturb her no longer. She had not, in any case, she suspected, very long to live. This afternoon, tired out, bathed in the fading sunshine, the pains in her back and at her heart gradually receding, she did not seem to care. If she had not long to live at least she would die then among friends, with Pip and her bit of amber and the long seashore and the rumble of the waves. . . .

She sank into a kind of doze, her head nodding forward on her breast, then woke with a start. What if she should have missed her train? She hastened up, dragging Pip after her. She hurried into the ticket office and, fumbling in her purse, said sharply through the little window:

"A third single to St. Lennan and a dog ticket, please."

There was a pause, and then a very abstracted voice answered her:

"Where did you say, madam?"

"St. Lennan, please—and a dog ticket."

The abstracted voice answered her, "No train to St. Lennan to-day. Last left ten minutes ago—3.5."

She had not heard. His words meant nothing.

"Third single to St. Lennan, please," she repeated.

A bearded, spectacled face appeared then at the window.

"No further train to St. Lennan to-day, madam. Last went ten minutes ago—3.5."

Fear surged down upon her. "Oh, but there

must be. I looked at the time-table. It said 3.30. Truly it did."

"Changed 1st of January. There *was* a 3.30. Changed to 3.5."

Terror had her by the throat. She stammered.

"Sorry, madam. No further trains to St. Lennan to-day."

The bearded face withdrew.

She turned round. A porter was passing. She stopped him. "Oh, porter, please, surely it can't be true. There *must* be a train to St. Lennan at 3.30."

He was a kindly man. He smiled at her genially. "Sorry, mum, changed 1st of January."

"Oh, what shall I do? What shall I do? It's dreadfully important I get there to-day. What *can* I do?"

"Well, mum, you could . . . let me see." He consulted the page of train times on the board. "Difficult place to get at, St. Lennan. You could take the 6 o'clock to Pentecost and catch the St. Borlase 4.30. No. You couldn't neither. That 'ud be too late. You could . . . I'm blowed if I see what you can do to-day, mum. There's the 6.30 to-morrow morning."

The 6.30 to-morrow morning! The 6.30 to-

morrow morning! What could she do? Sit in
the station all day and all night? She had not
money for an hotel. She had no friends. No
one. The only thing was to go back.

She stood looking out on to the station square
now quite deserted. Through the silence a sum-
mons as it were of fate came to her.

She bowed her head, and slowly, Pip close to
her side, she crossed the square.

CHAPTER IX

THE SENSE OF DANGER

M RS. AMOREST had recognised, as she walked up the High Street after leaving Mr. Agnew's office, that the hardest crisis of her life had come upon her. She met it almost as an old friend because she had been for so long expecting it. Like many other brave and spirited women it had always been the little things in life that had shown her weaknesses—to the big crises she had always risen as the swimmer braces himself for the crest of the green-towering wave. During the walk home she was dazed. Though she might have suspected the actual splendour of the annual thousand pounds, she had not in her heart doubted but that there would be a hundred or two—and a hundred or two would make all the difference.

And now there was nothing save a silver match-box!

Back in her own room, she seemed to be stand-

ing, precipitately, on the edge of a dark and
bottomless oubliette. What lay down there?
How deep was the fall? She realised with a
flash of surprise that for years now she had
expected that "one day her cousin would do
something for her." Although she had never
uttered the thought in outspoken words, she had
always, when funds were creeping so low as to
be almost invisible, known that at any rate there
was Cousin Francis. Now there was Cousin
Francis no longer.

It was fit and proper punishment for her. She
recognised that. The thought hurt her now
that her visits to her cousin had been frequent
only because she "had expectations." But she
was no sentimentalist. She did not allow herself
the luxury of self-chastisement without justifica-
tion. She had gone to see him because she was
fond of him, because she was sorry for him, and
because he was the only relation left to her in
the world save Brand. The only relation! She
could not have believed that his death—when
she had seen him so seldom—would make her
now so lonely. She wondered at her own loneliness. Why had she, when she was by nature
gregarious, loving her fellow beings, made no

real friends in the town? It was, she supposed, her pride, her dislike of revealing her poverty, her hesitation at being unable to return hospitality. But what would she give to have a true friend near her now!

After her conversation with Agatha Payne her courage for a moment failed her. She felt old and worn and desolate, and all that day she must clench her teeth and refuse to look either to the right or to the left. Beasts in the jungle on either side of her! Then, next morning at breakfast time, a marvellous thing occurred.

"There's a letter for you, mum, said Mrs. Bloxam, coming in with her hat askew and her accustomed air of bustling energy; "and that poor Miss Bellringer is terrible bad this morning. Suffering something cruel—and all because she would go to the station yesterday, against my advising her too!—there! and I shouldn't 'ave said nothing about it."

Mrs. Amorest took the letter and trembled through all her body. She did not hear Mrs. Bloxam's voice nor see the room nor the rain-driven day beyond the window pane. The letter was from her son.

The envelope was covered with stamps, addresses, inks blue and red and green, and that strangely mysterious and yet intimate handwriting conveying the information "not known here. Try Chester Street———"

She gazed at the envelope for a long time and, swimming up from beneath deep waters, murmured to her companion, "It's from my son, Mrs. Bloxam. At last, after two years."

Mrs. Bloxam paused, her arms akimbo. Her cheeks were suffused with generous pleasure.

"Is it really, mum? Well I never!"

At last, after gazing at the envelope for a long time, she had the courage to tear it apart. It was not a very long letter, but she caught it up and kissed it, then held it against her cheek.

The address was "Monterey, California," and then the date! She looked at it again and again to make certain that she was correct, pushing her reading spectacles up and down her nose. At last she said, "You look at that, Mrs. Bloxam. I make it out January 4, 1895. And this is February 1896. It must be wrong. The letter can't have been a whole year coming."

She would not allow the letter out of her hand, so Mrs. Bloxam leaned over her and studied it very carefully.

"I'm not a great 'and at reading, mum, if the truth be known, but that is certingly a 5——"

"A whole year!" Mrs. Amorest repeated. "Where can the letter have been?"

She read it then, and it was as follows:

DEAR OLD LADY—I can't pretend to have been much of a letter-writer during the last year, and I'm ashamed of myself. The truth is that I'd made an oath to myself not to let you know anything until I'd brought a deal off here. What I wanted to do was to make my pile, turn up unexpectedly in Cheltenham, give you the fright of your young life, and then make you a duchess, as you ought to be—but I've had the worst of bad luck over and over again. Tantalising isn't the word for it. If things hadn't at times gone so astonishingly well I'd have given it up and come home to England long ago, but I've so nearly brought it off once or twice that I can't make up my mind to leave it. I was on to a wonderful thing three months ago, and then what did I do but tumble down with diphtheria here in San Francisco, and another fellow got the chance.

I'm all right now, and there's some land prospecting down South, near a little place, Los Angeles (get out the map and look for it), that promises fine. Hold on for a while yet and I'll astonish you still one fine morning. I don't like to be beaten. I'm enclosing a photo I've had taken here. You'd hardly recognise your promising son, would you? I'm fit as anything now, and it may be it won't be long before you see me.

I was pleased to see from your last letter that you are keeping well and are happy. The address on your paper is Polchester. Don't know the place, but gather you are still living in Cheltenham. Isn't Polchester the place where there are some cousins of ours? Perhaps you're staying with them. You don't say. Glad you're stopping

on at Cheltenham, where you've got plenty of company.
Don't be lonely, old lady.

So long for the present, and look out for me any day.—
Your loving son,   BRAND.

She sighed deeply as she finished it. Then
she read it all through clearly.

"You see, Mrs. Bloxam," she said, as though
that lady had read the letter, "I did'nt want him
to think I'd left Cheltenham. It might have
fussed him. And I was thinking then I might
return there at any time. I left them this address
in the post office there. I don't know wherever
this letter can have been." She spelt out the
envelope again. "It's because he's written the
address so badly. Careless boy. "Try Chippen-
ham. Not known here." I should think not.
It must have been lying in the post office for
months. Isn't that too bad?"

Then she gazed and gazed at the photograph.
She would, of course, have known him anywhere.
But how he had filled out! How he had broad-
ened and thickened and strengthened! He
looked well. He was the handsomest man on
earth.

"He may come any minute, Mrs. Bloxam. I

knew he hadn't forgotten me, whatver they mignt say. He's coming back a rich man."

"Is he indeed, mum?" said Mrs. Bloxam. "And here's your tea, mum, and it'll all get cold if you don't drink it."

She lay back bathed in a luxury of happiness. She could think at first of nothing but her joy in being in touch with him once again. She lay there smiling, lost in happy dreams.

But when she had dressed, new thoughts came to her. That letter had been written a year ago. He had had diphtheria. What might not have happened in the intervening year? A whole year, and there had not been a line from him! That sense of fear she had had ever since her meeting with Mr. Agnew—a sense that some danger was tracking her and was drawing like a furtive but determined animal ever nearer and nearer—came close to her now. She was to be tantalised with the letter. It was to be a sign to her that she was never to see him again—his last farewell letter to her!

"What is the matter with me now?" she said to herself. "I was never like this before. Something new has come into this house. I never doubted but that he was coming back to me, and now, when I have his letter, at last after so long waiting, it seems to tell me I shall never see him again." She gazed and gazed at the photograph. "Oh, God! Give him back to me!" she prayed. "I don't think I can go on alone much longer. I'm so tired of being alone. Give him back to me!" and then, struggling against her stronger, more rebellious spirit, added, "Thy will be done."

Mrs. Bloxam came in very greatly disturbed. "There's that poor Miss Bellringer," she said, "crying something pitiful. She says she's frightened of something. Mrs. Payne 'as been in and upset 'er. She says it's 'er 'eart, and 'er back's 'urting something shameful. Poor worm! She's not long for this world, if you're asking my opinion."

Mrs. Amorest was not herself feeling her strongest. All the excitement of the last two days and the lack of sleep had made her, as she used chaffingly to confess to her friends, "a little weak in the knee." But the sight of Mrs. Bloxam's good-natured face so truly disturbed touched her deeply. She went at once, crossing the passage, into May Beringer's room.

Entering, she was aware sharply once more of a sense of danger. She was not an imaginative woman nor one given to nervous fears; she had pluck and courage fortified by utter belief in powers that could put all the battalions of evil to ignominious flight, but she was weary and unstrung. She stopped on the threshold. Her eyes went instinctively, as though they were guided, to the mantelpice. The red amber was not there. She looked then at the bed. Miss Beringer, propped with pillows, was sitting up, her woollen waistcoat tied by the sleeves around her thin and bony neck. Her long, flushed face was yellow and drawn. One arm was thrown over the dog, which, lying full length on the bed, was crouched close to her side; in the other she held the red amber.

Mrs. Bloxam, standing beside the bed, was uttering consoling words and offering some beef-tea on the little battered black-japanned tray. The fire was not lit. The room was very cold and dark. "Now do, my dear," Mrs. Bloxam was saying, "drink this nice beef-tea. You'll feel a different woman when you've drunk it. I'll take the dog for a run."

"No," said Miss Beringer, holding the dog closer to her. "You've taken him out once this morning, thank you. I don't wish him to go again. Thank you very much." She drank the beef-tea as though she were thinking of something else.

"Well, if you don't mind me saying so, miss," continued Mrs. Bloxam, "it really isn't. 'ealthy to 'ave that dog on the bed with you. It isn't really, miss, Not that it isn't a clean little dog, but dogs is dogs."

"No, thank you, Mrs. Bloxam."

"And 'ere's Mrs. Hamorest come to cheer you up. Why, bless you, you'll be right as tuppence to-morrow, you see if you ain't. Don't you let yourself get down'earted. Keep up your spirits. The sun will be shining to-morrer mornin'."

"Thank you, Mrs. Bloxam, I'm sure it will," answered Miss Beringer patiently.

"Is there anything else I can do for you while I'm at it? I'll just be getting Bloxam's dinner and I'll be back in a jiffy."

"Thank you, Mrs. Bloxam. There's nothing else I want, thank you." Mrs. Bloxam departed. Mrs. Amorest came then and, drawing a chair, sat down beside the bed.

"Do you mind my coming in for a little?" she asked. "You needn't talk if you don't want to.

I always think a little company's pleasant when you are not feeling well."

"But I do want to talk," May Beringer said. She put the piece of amber on the bed beside her and caught Mrs. Amorest's hand. "Do you mind my holding your hand? Do say if you mind."

"Why, of course not," Mrs. Amorest said gently. "Now tell me what's the matter. Don't you think you ought to see a doctor?"

"A doctor can't do anything." Her hand shook in Mrs. Amorest's grasp. "It's that woman next door who's killing me."

"What woman? Mrs. Payne?"

"Yes." May Beringer's voice sank to a whisper. "Speak softly. She can hear what we say."

"But of course she can't," Mrs. Amorest reassured her. "There's a thick wall between."

"No, but she can. Walls are nothing to her. It's fate. She's going to finish me. She made me miss that train yesterday."

"What train?"

"I was going away and I got to the station and I missed the train. She knew I'd come back."

But this was not at all the kind of talk with which Mrs. Amorest's clear, cool brain could have patience. "Now that's really nonsense," she said, smiling and patting May Beringer's hand; "you're ill or you wouldn't have ideas like that in your head. You've had ideas about Mrs. Payne since the first moment you saw her. Of course Mrs. Payne is a little odd. She's not quite like other women, but she doesn't mean any harm. Why, I've lived in this house for months and months with her and she's never done any one any harm."

"That's because," May Beringer whispered feverishly, "you haven't got anything that she wants."

"What do you mean?" asked Mrs. Amorest, feeling in spite of herself the darkness of the room and a kind of foggy chill that seemed to hang like a mist about the bed.

"It's my piece of amber she wants," May Beringer went on, "and she's not going to have it. Never, never, never! Not if I die to prevent her."

Mrs. Amorest leaned forward and stroked her friend's forehead. "Dear Miss Beringer, you mustn't imagine things like that. Truly, it's only because you're not well. Now let me arrange your pillows and make you more comfortable."

May Beringer began to cry, a weak helpless sobbing. "You don't understand," she said, as the tears trickled down her cheeks. "You think it's absurd because you don't know how people can want things. You're good, and you wouldn't take anything that belongs to somebody else. But she's bad, and she isn't right in her head either. She was in here and said if I gave it her she would leave me alone."

"She was in here? When was that?"

"The night before last. That's why I meant to go away. She frightened me so! Oh! you don't know how frightening she can be when she looks at you with her black eyebrows and smiles. She is going to kill me if she can't get it!"

Mrs. Amorest looked about the room, her small lined face wrinkled with surprise. "She said that? That she would leave you alone if you gave her that piece of amber?"

"Yes, she did indeed. She's quite crazy to have it. She says it belonged to her before it belonged to me—as though dear Jane didn't give it to me after buying it herself from Mr. Faithorner in Exeter."

"Then she must be mad—mad, and wicked too." Mrs. Amorest was trembling with indignation. "Why, that's as bad as being a thief!"

"She *is* a thief," said May Beringer. "She'd take it at once if I were alone in the house. But she knows that Mrs. Bloxam and you know it's mine. She *is* a thief."

"I can't understand it," Lucy Amorest went on, "any one wanting anything like that. Of course I like to have nice things, but I wouldn't *take* anybody's. . . . Why, it's truly wicked! And that's only a bit of stone or something. It isn't as though it were alive. What is it made of really?"

"I don't know," said May Beringer, looking at it tenderly as it lay there on the counterpane. "I think the Chinese find it on the seashore or something. But I'm not certain about its not being alive. You will think me very silly, Mrs. Amorest, but I'm an old woman and have lived a long time, and I sometimes think that things are more alive than people. When you've put a lot of feeling into something, don't you give it a sort of life? It may be grateful, you know, for your being so fond of it.

"Of course that's very fanciful, and perhaps it

isn't very religious, but one gets queer fancies when one's old. Jane (she was my dear friend, you know) said when she gave it me that it had some of her heart in it, and I think perhaps it has. I know that wicked woman can kill me first before she gets it from me."

She was trembling all over, and Lucy Amorest, touched with pity, put her arm about the thin bony body.

"Now you're not going to feel frightened any more. I'm here, and I won't let her touch you. I'm going to speak to her and give her a piece of my mind."

"Oh no, you mustn't do that." May Beringer sat straight up in bed. "You don't know what she will do to you. You mustn't, indeed you mustn't."

Lucy Amorest smiled.

"She can't hurt me, dear. There is Some One will protect us both, stronger than Agatha Payne. Now how do you feel in general? Is your back hurting you?"

"It isn't my back so much as my heart. Put your hand here and just feel how it jumps." Mrs. Amorest placed her hand against May Beringer's breast and felt the strange irregular

beat—it seemed to jump like an animal impris-
oned and then altogether to die away.

"Well, I think you ought to see a doctor," she
said, nodding her head decisively. "I know a very
nice one, let me tell him to come in this afternoon."

But May Beringer shook her head vigorously.

"No, no," she said; "I had a doctor once in
Exeter and he said I must wear spectacles, and
so I did for two years, and there wasn't anything
the matter with my eyes at all. I don't believe
doctors know a thing more than we do ourselves.
They are all humbugs, if you ask me."

She was energetic; there was some colour now
in her cheeks; Lucy Amorest's visit had done her
good.

"I must leave you now for a little. I'll come
back in the afternoon."

"Oh, you will, won't you?" May Beringer's
eyes were beseeching. "You are so good to me.
I'm sure I don't know why."

"Nonsense." Lucy Amorest bent down and
kissed her. "You sleep for a little and you'll
feel ever so much better."

"I don't want to sleep. I have such dreams."

"You won't this time. You try and see."

She went back to her room and thought it out. Her principal feeling was one of anger and indignation with Agatha Payne. She had never heard anything so wicked and so cruel. To frighten and bully that poor old thing simply because she wanted that toy!

The fact that May Beringer had really been to the station and tried to escape by the train brought it all home to her most vividly. Never would she have embarked on such an adventure had she not been most truly frightened—frightened by that wicked old woman!

Lucy Amorest ate her frugal luncheon, then knocked at Agatha Payne's door. There was no answer, so she waited for a little, then knocked again. Now there was some sound from within and she entered.

The atmosphere was so close that she stayed for a moment by the door. A very large fire was burning. The room was exceedingly hot. Agatha Payne was sitting at the table playing cards. She gazed intensely. She did not look up. Her lips moved. She sat hunched, her dress pulled up to her knees. Her hands, holding a card, hung hovering over the table. Mrs. Amorest was frightened. For some unaccountable reason she wanted to turn and go straight back to her room again. She had never been frightened in Mrs. Payne's room before. It was perhaps the heat and absence of any air.

"Excuse me, Agatha," she said. "I want to speak to you a moment."

Mrs. Payne did not look up. She bent forward, touching the cards as they lay on the table. This angered Mrs. Amorest. She forgot her fear. She came forward, close to the table.

"Excuse me," she said again, "but I *must* speak to you. It is something of importance."

Mrs. Payne laid the card in her hand carefully on the table, then looked up.

"What is it?" she asked.

"How strange she looks! Mrs. Amorest thought. Her large black eyes, dull like pools of ink, were expressionless. Her big heavy body was lurched together as though with a slight push it would tumble forward and lie, like a heap of clothes, on the floor. She had the air of some one who had been drinking.

"I have been seeing Miss Beringer," Mrs. Amorest said. "She is very ill—very seriously ill."

"What have I to do with her?" asked Mrs.

Payne. Her body was galvanised into energy. She turned round in her chair and her eyes filled with a strange brooding expectancy; life had struck there as light strikes a pool.

"You have this to do with her," said Mrs. Amorest indignantly, "that you have been in there and something you have said to her has frightened her. She is easily frightened, and her heart is bad. You must leave her alone or I will have a doctor here who will make you."

"Indeed!" said Agatha Payne, looking at the little woman with a deep and slow contempt. "Who says that I have frightened her?"

"She says so herself. She has an idea in her head that you want to steal something of hers. I can't believe that of you, but sick women have strange fancies. She has done you no harm. Why won't you leave her alone?"

"Leave her alone!" Mrs. Payne laughed. "The silly old fool! Silly old fools both of you. A pair of sentimental old women. You with your precious boy and she with her dog!" She turned contemptuously back to her cards.

Mrs. Amorest flushed angrily.

"You leave my son alone," she answered.

"And you leave Miss Beringer alone too. From what she tells me, you're no better than a thief."

"Thief, is it?" said Agatha Payne, looking at the cards. "Now you leave me alone, Lucy Amorest, and mind your own business, or it will be the worse for you."

"It *is* my own business!" Mrs. Amorest answered. "The woman is sick and has no one to care for her. If you go near her room again I'll—I'll call for the police!"

"You will, will you?" Mrs. Payne laughed. "And what have the police to do with it? You'd look fine and silly with the police coming in. You'd have them arrest me, I suppose? And for what? For going into that idiot's room to see whether she wanted anything! That's all I get for my kindness!"

Sho got up slowly from the table and moved over to the fire. Her thick heavy body seemed to tower over the rest of the room.

"Now, look here, Lucy Amorest, she said, "you mind your own business. I've stood you long enough—poking your nose in here where you are not wanted. I've not interfered with you, have I? Well then, leave me to myself."

"You may say what you like to me," Mrs.

Amorest answered. "I'm not afraid of you, but
that poor woman's life is in danger. Give her
another fright and with her heart as it is anything can happen, and then you will be a murderess as well as a thief . . . !"

She paused, her breast heaving with indignation.

Agatha Payne seemed to quieten. She stared
beyond Mrs. Amorest to the far spaces of the
room. "She is so bad as that, is she?" she said
gruffly. "Well—what does it matter? You are
sentimental, Lucy, as always. She is old; she is
sick; she is penniless. We are all old and sick
and penniless. Three old, sick, penniless women.
Do you know that? There are other old women,
thousands of them, who have homes and friends
and money. Perhaps they are happier than us,
perhaps they are not. Perhaps, although they
have all those things, there are others who are
waiting for them to die, waiting for their places.
They are tiresome; they have memories only of a
time that others do not know. They admire
things that all the others think absurd. With
old age it is always the same. After seventy the
sooner you go the better. With every one it is
so, but with us! How sentimental to pretend

that we should live! We are not happy; we make no one else happy. This old woman in the next room, she is always complaining and crying and suffering. It would be a kindness if I were to go now, put my hand around her neck and choke her. You believe in another life where she will be happy and play on a harp, and yet you hinder her from going there. It is your senti- ment. But in the end you are more cruel than I."

"You speak like that," said Lucy Amorest, "and yet, although you are old like her, you would give everything to have something of hers, a piece of coloured stone that is nothing— nothing at all."

"Speak of what you understand," Agatha answered almost amiably. "What do you know of lust or desire for anything? You have never felt passion with your milk-and-water religion and your sentimentality. If I were to know that I had only half an hour more to live, I would want the sensation of owning that beautiful thing. Beauty! You don't know the meaning of the word."

She slumped down into the rocking-chair and with her back to Mrs. Amorest rocked there, kicking her shoe in the air.

To that broad back bulging between the bars of the chair, Lucy delivered her last words: "You must leave her alone. Whether I am sentimental or not, I will see to that." Then she left the room.

She felt the cool, even chilly air of the passage refreshing after that close heat. She would not think of herself. There was something in that woman's words that had struck deep into her heart, but that she kept away from her. She was tired, worn out. She went into her room and, lying down, slept. It was evening when she woke. Her room was dark. She stared about her at first, not remembering where she was. Then recollecting, she started up, blaming herself that she had neglected that poor woman. She lit her candles, brushed her hair and washed her face. She took a story of Grace Aguilar's from the shelf, then hurried into the other room.

May Beringer was lying down, the piece of amber in her hand, Pip beside her. The room was cold and had a faint thin light.

"Oh, I am so sorry," Mrs. Amorest cried, "I have been so long away. How are you now? Better?"

"I tried to get up but my back hurt so," Miss

Beringer's tearful voice answered her. "I thought you were never coming."

Soon Mrs. Amorest had made the room bright again. The fire was lit. The candles shone. The kettle boiled and there was a hot cup of tea. But May Beringer's face did not change. She seemed for ever to be listening for something. She drank the tea, suffered her pillows to be shaken and her sheets smoothed.

Then Mrs. Amorest sat down beside the bed. "Now," she said, "that's better. I have brought a book I thought you might like. Such a pretty story. Do you like to be read to?"

"Yes," said May Beringer.

"Shall I read a little of it?"

"Yes, please. You don't hear anything, do you?"

"Hear anything? No, of course not. Now I'll begin. Are you quite comfortable?"

"Yes, thank you."

"Chapter one. . . ."

CHAPTER X

DEATH OF MAY BERINGER

THE firelight made patterns on the wall. Lucy Amorest's voice rose and fell. May Beringer lay without moving, staring in front of her.

The words began to swim before the reader's eyes. The print in patterns of grey and black and ivory thickened like swarms of flies across the light. The head nodded. The book crashed to the floor.

"Oh! I beg your pardon," Mrs. Amorest cried. "Reading aloud always after a time makes me sleepy. And I expect that it is making you sleepy too. You've had enough of it, I'm sure."

May Beringer did not reply. She was striving to be brave enough to utter certain words. What she wanted to say was: "Please, Mrs. Amorest, don't leave me to-night. I'm sure you could make yourself comfortable with the armchair and the other chair. I will never forget it if you stay. Only for to-night. Please, please don't leave me alone."

That was what she wanted to say. For the last hour she had not been listening to the words that were read, but had been forming these words in her brain. "Oh, please, Mrs. Amorest . . ."

But she had not the courage to utter them. She was frightened about this, as she was frightened about everything else in her life. She had detected in Mrs. Amorest something, not precisely hard, but rather restrained and critical. Mrs. Amorest would think May Beringer a fool for her fears, and although she did not mind that she should be thought a fool could she only get her way, the immediate moment when she would make her suggestion and then see that look in Mrs. Amorest's eyes was too difficult for her. She rehearsed the words to herself again and again but the pushing them from silence into sound was too difficult for her.

And yet that awful moment when she should be left alone with all the long night in front of her was terrible for her too. Every way there was fear. That woman was waiting for her on the other side of the wall. She could see her standing there, listening, waiting until Mrs.

Amorest should be gone. Oh! if only Mrs. Amorest would, herself, propose that she should stay.

She read on and on until May Beringer could have screamed from irritation. It wasn't that silly book that she wanted to hear, but rather those blessed words, "Wouldn't you like me to stay here to-night? I could make myself quite comfortable on that chair . . ." The book fell to the floor; the moment of departure had arrived.

Mrs. Amorest rose from her chair and gave a little yawn. "Why, how late it is! I've been reading a long time. Don't you think that's a very pretty story?"

"Yes."

"I like the way she writes, don't you?"

"Yes, I do."

"We'll have some more to-morrow. I've quite forgotten how the story goes. It must be a long long time since I read it."

And May Beringer was saying, "Oh, do say you'll stop with me. Stop with me at least until I have fallen asleep." She struggled to have the courage to force out the words:

"Don't you think . . . ?"

"What is it, dear?"

". . . you could make up the fire a little before you go?"

"Why, of course I will."

Mrs. Amorest made up the fire, patted the pillows a little, then kissed May Beringer. "Now are you sure you are comfortable? Your heart isn't troubling you so much, is it?"

"No, oh no!" She put out her hand and drew Mrs. Amorest to the bed.

"Do stay with me a moment longer. I don't want you to go."

"Why, of course I will, dear."

"You don't think me foolish, do you?"

"Of course not."

"I am foolish and frightened. A silly old woman. But you've been so kind to me. There's one thing I'd like you to do."

"What is it, dear?"

"Would you mind, before you go, saying a prayer, a prayer about the dangers of the night and being kept safe?"

Mrs. Amorest nodded her head. "I know," she said. She knelt down beside the bed and closed her eyes. Still holding May Beringer's hand, she prayed:

"Dear Lord Jesus, we are Thy children and

Thou knowest what is best for us. We pray Thee now when the night comes down over our heads and there is darkness everywhere that Thy might may be ever before our eyes, and that whether we are waking or sleeping we may know no fear. The powers of darkness are obedient to Thy command. Our trust is in Thee, and because Thou lovest Thy children Thou wilt give them nothing that can do them harm. So trusting, we fall asleep in Thy arms, dear Jesus. Amen."

"What a nice prayer," May Beringer said with a sigh. "I have never heard it before."

"Yes, it is a nice one," said Mrs. Amorest. "Our nurse used to say it to us when we were children."

"Where did you live when you were a child?" asked May Beringer, holding Mrs. Amorest's hand very tightly.

"We lived in the Lake District," said Mrs. Amorest, smiling. "Near Keswick."

"Were you happy as a child?"

"Very happy. My father was a clergyman. We had very little money, but we didn't want much. There were three of us and we lived all day on the hills. We used to walk for ever and

ever. We knew all the hills and all the lakes.
Scawfell and Great Gable and Cat Bells and
Crummock and Buttermere and St. John's Vale
and Wastdale Head and Grasmere." She said
the names over slowly, tasting them on her
tongue. "And I have never been back there. If
I could once more see Thirlmere from Helvellyn——" She broke off, laughing. "I forget I'm an old woman. I couldn't climb even
Helvellyn now. I've loved Glebeshire and Corn-
wall and Devonshire since, but not as I loved
those hills."

"Doesn't it always rain up there?" May
Beringer asked. "I've heard it does." And
behind these words the others were following:
"Oh, please stay here with me to-night! Please
stay here with me to-night." But she could not
force them. They would not come.

"No, of course it does not. That's only the
silly nonsense that people talk. There is a lot
of rain in all parts of England, but we used to
love when we were children to see the storms
come up over the hills, hiding them, and then
breaking like paper and letting the light come
through. And the Lake—Derwentwater—you
should see the colour run over it like some one

dancing. I wrote poetry about it when I was a girl, and then I married a poet, which was better than writing poetry."

May Beringer stared desperately about her. Was there nothing that would put it into Mrs. Amorest's head to stay?

"Well," said Mrs. Amorest, gently withdrawing her hand, "I must go now. You must have a long sleep and then you'll see how much better you'll be in the morning."

"Won't you stay a little?"

"No. You must go to sleep now." She bent down and kissed her. "Go to sleep and have beautiful dreams."

"Oh, please stay a little while." But Mrs. Amorest was gone.

Mrs. Amorest was gone, and in the silence that followed her departure there came a new sound that May had never heard in that house before. It was the dripping of a tap. It must be out there on the landing. How clearly it came through the closed door. Like some one counting time. One, two, three, four—then a pause— then several drips together. Like an old man querulously complaining, and then in the steady drip, drip again something stern and remorseless.

Some one counting as though he said, "Now when I've reached thirty . . ."

May began to count. She counted to ten, and after that so many came together that she could count no longer. She would never sleep with that horrible thing at her door. The fantastic idea came to her—and one's ideas are fantastic when one is sick and has been lying in bed with so many idle thoughts hovering about one—that that horrible woman had started the noise. It would be like her. There would be other noises also in the house that would be of her agency. Oh! I must escape from this! I must! I will go into Mrs. Amorest's room and never mind if she thinks me a fool. I will tell her that I must stay with her, that I won't be alone. . . .

She moved, got half out of bed; but her head was swimming. The room danced round and round her. Pip climbed off the bed, gave her one beseeching look, and crawled away out of sight.

That frightened her. He had been so strange during these last two days, as though he also was sick, nervous, and frightened, refusing his food. Even Mrs. Bloxam had noticed it.

She sank back upon the pillows again, and

thence weakly cried, "Pip! Pip! Come back. Come here. Good dog! Good dog!" But Pip did not reappear.

A curious lethargy slipped upon her. It was as though something had seized her limbs and she would never be able to move again. She was almost asleep and fancied through her half-closed eyes that figures moved dimly about the room. She was in her childhood once more; all the family were round her with their noise and their selfishness and their jokes, in which, for some reason, she was never able to share. There was Gertrude, her eldest sister, with her large fishy eyes, her thin frizzled hair; always trying to marry Somebody. May hated Gertrude and Gertrude hated May. Gertrude was for ever putting her in her place, telling her not to do this, not to go there, not to be such a silly. May could hear her voice very plainly, that shrill high voice saying, "Don't be such a silly, May. Isn't May a silly?" And she was a silly—for ever doing the wrong thing. Had Gertrude been kind to her and shown her how to do things it would have been different. If Gertrude had been kind to her as Jane Betts (afterwards) was, what a bright happy woman May would have become. But they were always laughing at her, so that, although May was in any case a clumsy and awkward girl, she was yet more clumsy and awkward. Well, Gertrude was dead now. Dead. May had beaten her there. But was she dead? Was she not standing there by the fireplace in just that lilac-coloured dress she used to wear, with just that same affected smile? And there was Rupert, fat and red-faced. How anxious Rupert had been about his figure! But it was difficult because he loved food, and he would starve himself for a week and then break down and eat more than ever. But he had been kind to her when he remembered, only he did not remember very often. He was kind to her, but he despised her. May tried all things to make him despise her less. She wanted some one to be proud of her. Some one. Any one. Their stupid ignorant governesses. Miss Marchmont. Miss LeFevre. Miss Albany. May remembered them all although it was so long ago. But it was not so long ago after all. It was only the other day. Was not that Miss Marchmont there now, standing in the corner near the door?

Miss Marchmont was the thin bony one with the flat bit on the end of her nose which somebody said was like the portraits of Rembrandt, so that after that they always called her "Miss Rembrandt," and didn't she hate it! Surely it was only yesterday that Miss Marchmont had been seen coming into the house at five in the morning and had been compelled to leave that very day! How excited they had all been and how curious! What had she been doing that she should stay out all night? The girls had talked among themselves, and even May had been admitted into the family councils. The boys had known more than the girls did, and hinted at what they knew but wouldn't tell . . . And there was May's mother—there just beyond the railings of the bed. How May had adored her, and how she had longed to be adored in return! But it was always the other girls who were petted and praised and shown off in company. May had done things that she was sure her mother would like, and her mother would have liked them too had only Gertrude or Clara or Isabella done them, but because it was May . . .

Her mother had not been happy. May saw that now. She had found her once crying in her bedroom and had longed to put her arm around her and console her, but she had not known how to do it nor what to say. She had failed in that, as she had failed in everything else in her life. The shadows moved and moved again. The fire leapt and fell. May slept. She dreamed. She was hurrying along a windy road. It was night, and on one side of her was a dark wood. She was frightened, of course, and she knew that when she came to a cross-roads some one would be there waiting for her. Some one terrible. She did not want to go on. She tried to stop, but the wind drove her along. Had she more courage she would run into the wood and hide there, but no, she must go on faster and faster. The cross-roads were there, and standing clearly to be seen in the pale light was some one waiting for her. She was flung onwards crying for mercy. She tried to turn back, and then as she saw the hands stretched out to grasp her she woke. She lay, the sweat on her forehead, her body trembling, her heart running and jumping and missing, and missing and jumping and running. She could see quite clearly. There were no longer any shadows in the room. She heard, so plainly that it seemed that it must be with her now beside her bed, the running tap. One, two, three, four. . . . She lay, trying to remember Mrs.

Amorest's prayer. "Lord Jesus, Lord Jesus, Lord Jesus," she repeated.

She closed her eyes, but a sound forced her to open them again. She cried, "Who's there?" The handle of the door was turning. Very carefully and quietly, closing the door behind her, Agatha Payne came in.

"Good evening, Miss Beringer," she said. "I came in to see whether you wanted anything."

"I want nothing." With a great effort, breaking the restraint that held her, she turned and lay with her face towards the wall.

Agatha Payne sat down on the chair beside the bed. "But I want us to have a little talk. If you are sleepy, I can wait. I am not at all sleepy myself."

May neither answered nor moved. A long silence followed, and for May it was filled with an agonising determination not to show her fear. She would not move; she would not speak. She was biting her lips, her hands were fiercely clenched, one holding tightly the red amber. That woman might kill her but she would not move. Then her heart ceased to beat. It ceased absolutely. She began to suffocate. Some one seemed to be pushing her up to the wall so that her face was pressed against the faded wall-paper. She could not endure her suffering and she turned in the bed.

That woman was sitting quietly on the chair. She was wearing a loose wrapper of a dirty yellow; one end of the wrapper had slipped off her shoulder, revealing it of a curious copper brown colour, and part of her breast. She sat leaning forward a little, staring at the counter-pane.

On seeing Miss Beringer turn she asked, smiling:

"Why do you complain about me?"

"I haven't complained."

"Yes. To Mrs. Amorest. She came into my room and was very insulting. I'm sure I've been very kind to you. There are not many who would bother about a miserable sick old woman like yourself."

"Oh, go away. Please, please go away!" May Beringer whispered.

"Go away? Oh no! I am very comfortable here. I shall stay for half an hour or an hour, or perhaps two. Perhaps all night."

"I know. You have come to steal my amber from me."

"Steal? Oh no—certainly not. I have come to make you more comfortable. To smooth your pillows!"

She leant over the bed.

May Beringer gave a little cry half-strangled by her fear and shuddered to the wall. "Don't touch me! Don't touch me! I'll scream. I'll rouse everybody. Don't touch me!"

Agatha Payne, holding her wrapper about her brown neck with one hand, leaned over her. Her hair, raven black in the firelight, had loosened and some of it hung untidily about her face.

"Your screams won't be heard. There's only old Lucy Amorest. She's fast asleep by this time, and there's the passage between. Besides, you can't scream. You're too frightened. Try and see. But I have not come to hurt you. Only to spend an hour or two. You go to sleep. I shan't touch you. What do you think I am, a murderess?"

"Yes, you would murder me to have my amber."

"Murder! That's a nasty word. Why don't you take things more quietly? See! I'm sitting down. I'm kind enough if you know how to deal with me, but when you tremble like that it gives me pleasure. Can't you understand? The more you tremble the more I like to tease you. I lift my hand, and see!—you shake all over!"

"Can't you see that I'm sick?" May Beringer whispered. "I'm not young any more. My heart's bad, and my back. It's true that you frighten me. Everything always has. You did from the first moment I saw you."

"Well, well," said Agatha Payne, moving her hand slowly up and down the counterpane. "Fancy that! I wonder why. Of course I'm not very handsome, and sometimes I think I'm not quite right in the head. I've had a good deal to try me at times. But you shouldn't tempt me. I'd have been quiet enough if you hadn't shaken and quivered at the mere sight of me. That would excite anybody."

She looked at her, huddled up beneath the clothes, crouching as though fearing a blow. "You're a miserable old woman, aren't you? We aren't much, the three of us up here at the top of this house. Birds of a feather!

"But at least Lucy Amorest's got some spirit. You haven't the spirit of a flea. Why, if I were to drag you out of your bed, strip you naked, and beat you round the room, you wouldn't object."

"That's what you want," said May Beringer, panting. "You want my piece of amber. You'll have to kill me to get it."

Agatha Payne shrugged her shoulders. "I'll have it some day, never you fear. Now, why don't you give it me quietly? It's only a toy when all's said. Or suppose we share it? I have it a month and you have it a month. Let's look at it."

"No, no, no!"

"All right, then. I can wait."

She sat in silence for a little and then she went on: "What do you cling to life for? You're sick and always in pain. You've got no money. You haven't a friend in the world. I've at least got my passions, and Lucy Amorest's got her pluck. But you! You'll be happier dead—far happier."

May Beringer began to cry. "You're cruel to me—dreadfully cruel. What have I ever done to you? You are the cruellest woman I have ever known. To-morrow morning I'll have you turned out of the house. I'll tell them all what you are doing to me."

"And what am I doing, pray? Having a little chat. Looking after you a little. Crying? What do you do that for? Don't you know it excites me? Crying? I've never cried in my life, not when my lover left me because he was tired of me. You've never had a lover, not with that face of yours. But I had—plenty once. I was handsome, and I didn't care what I did. You! You snivelling old scarecrow! It would be a fine sort of man that would make love to *you!*"

May Beringer sat up, a strange sight with the tears drying on her cheeks and her grey hair hanging about her face. She kept her hands beneath the sheets.

"I beg you to leave me just for to-night," she said. "You can do what you like in the morning—I won't tell any one—but for to-night . . ."

"Yes," said Agatha Payne, "give me that piece of amber and I'll go."

"No. Never. Jane gave it me."

"Very well, then. I'll wait a little. I don't care. I can sit up all night if need be."

She gave a little shiver. "It's cold in here. You've let the fire almost out. I'll have a blaze in a minute."

She went over to the fire, shovelled on the coal from the scuttle, found a piece of newspaper which she held up, going down on her knees.

The room was for a moment dark, then a golden light sprang up behind the newspaper, there was a roaring chuckle and the fire was ablaze. Agatha stayed there on her knees before the glow.

She liked the heat, she knelt there, her hands spread out fan-wise. The fire, brilliant now and leaping, changed the room. Great shadows were thrown on the walls—Agatha's hand was gigantic like a flat moving fish. The only candle was near its end, and leapt also as though it were emulating the fire, throwing its own shadows in silly rivalry. Agatha knelt without speaking, and in the silence May Beringer heard very clearly the dripping, drunken voice of the tap: "One . . . two . . . five . . . I sh . . . hate . . . I . . shall . . . get . . . it . . . for being . . . late one—two—three—four. . . ."

She had her idea. While that woman had her back toward her she would slip from the bed, run across the passage, and escape into Mrs. Amorest's room. It was as though she were attempting the most dangerous feat of her life. She half rose, drew her knees together, slid to the other side of the bed, had her feet on the floor.

Instantly Agatha Payne turned. "Hullo! What are you about?"

May Beringer stayed frozen, her body limply attached to the bed. She had even now her chance. The door was not far. Once in the passage she could at least cry out so that Mrs. Amorest would wake and hear her. But she could not move. For one thing her legs were trembling so pitifully that they would not support her body and she was almost slipping to the floor. She could only gaze miserably upon that woman, still kneeling but turning her great shapeless body towards her, the blazing fire giving her black hair a glittering sheen.

"I was going for a moment," May Beringer whispered, "into the passage."

"No, I think not." Agatha Payne slowly rose, looking steadily at her. "If you want anything I can get it for you." Then her expression changed. "Ah! So you have it in your hand. I wondered where it was."

May Beringer put the hand that clutched the amber behind her back. "Ah! let me go! Please let me go!" she whispered.

"I should think not." She took a step towards her. "You'll catch your death all naked. You get back into bed. I'm mistress here now. You want looking after, I can see." She made another slow lurching step towards her. May Beringer could not take her eyes from that face, nor that shining hair, nor that shapeless body. She crept back into bed and crouched there, her grey hair now all about her eyes, staring through her hair, the bed-clothes huddled about her.

Agatha Payne came over and sat down in the chair once more. "So that's what you were up to, was it? Escaping into the passage ill as you are. I can see you're not safe to be left. A nice report I must give to the doctor to-morrow when I've let you wander all over the house."

May could only stare and stare; her breathing came in pants. Her body gave little jerks from time to time as though it were trying to shake from itself some dreadful weight. Her face was of a grey ivory shadow. Only her eyes, terrified, peered out like some one staring into the dark.

The candle gave a leap and went out.

"So you're holding it there under the bed-clothes, are you?" Agatha Payne went on. "That's a childish thing. Like a schoolgirl. Give it me for a moment. I'll return it to you."

"No," came a small dry voice as though from an infinite distance, "I won't."

"Oh, you won't, won't you?" Agatha sucked her finger reflectively. "Perhaps I shall have to make you. In spite of my affection for you, I don't think I *can* sit here all night. You'd much better give it me and have done with it. You'll have to tell them in the morning that you've given it me, or I'll come in to-morrow night too— and the night after that and the night after that until you *do* give it me. What a fuss to make about a little thing! I'm a determined woman. I always have my way in the end. You'd much better give it me and go to sleep quietly."

The voice came again dry and distant, "Jane gave it me."

"Oh, she did, did she? You've told me that before. You haven't seen your Jane for years, and I'm sure she's forgotten all about you long ago. Do you know that when you're dead there's not a single soul will be sorry? That's a nice thought, isn't it? But I don't want to be un-kind. If you weren't such a poor miserable creature I wouldn't bother with you, but you excite me. I like to see you cry. I like to see you tremble. Now, you'd better give it me or I shall have to take it."

The voice came again, "I won't. Jane gave it me."

"Now, come on. Give it up." Agatha leant over the bed. May Beringer with a little strangled cry moved towards the wall.

Agatha Payne moved her hand, and, quite gently, touched May Beringer's shoulder. "I'm not going to hurt you, but I'm going to have that piece of amber—just because I said I would. Come now."

Great shivers shook May Beringer's body. Two tears welled into her eyes and then slowly trickled on to her dry cheeks.

"Come, give it me."

Still gently she shook the other's shoulder. Then something moved in her, some sudden passion or fury. She leaned right over the bed, her wrapper slipping, her hair loose and wild.

"You silly fool, don't aggravate me. I *shall* hurt you if you don't take care. Give it up now. Give it up." May Beringer was pressed against the wall but her head was turned, staring up into Agatha's.

"Are you going to let me have it? I shan't

ask you again." There was no reply, only a long-drawn heaving sigh.

Agatha Payne stretched her arm across the other's body, reached down below the clothes, and pulled at the hand. May Beringer drew herself up over the pillow against the iron bars of the bed. Her body shook. Her lips were drawn back. Between her set teeth came little shuddering sobs.

"Now, then, don't be a fool any longer. You see I mean what I say." Their faces now were almost touching. Agatha's hand pulled at the clenched fist. She felt the cool of the amber. With a rough, strong movement she pushed up May Beringer's arm.

At the same moment it was as though some sudden shock galvanised May's body. She rose straight up against the wall, stiffly like a rod, her eyes staring out over the fire-shadowed room. A convulsive movement shuddered through her. She whispered, "Oh, Jesus! Jesus!" then with a sigh collapsed against Agatha Payne's bare breast.

The hand was still tightly clenched. Agatha took the amber, then, drawing back, saw the body slide under the bed-clothes huddled in a heap, but the head, with staring eyes, rested on the pillow.

May Beringer was dead. There was no doubt of it.

Agatha drew back, holding the amber in one hand, folding the wrapper over her with the other.

"I didn't mean that!" she whispered huskily. "I didn't mean that!" There was a sound at her feet. The dog crept from under the bed and looked up at her. She looked down on him, then stood stroking the amber with her hand. She went back to the bed, smoothed the counterpane. The body lay now as though it were asleep, only the eyes were wide. She stood thinking. She went to the mantelpiece, placed the amber upon it, then very quietly stole from the room.

CHAPTER XI

IT was of course Mrs. Bloxam who in the morning first learnt of poor Miss Beringer's death. She came tumbling into Mrs. Amorest's room: "Oh, mum! Poor Miss Bellringer! It's 'appened just as I thought. Lyin' as though she'd just dropped off in 'er sleep, pore worm, and nobody by 'er. A peaceful death that's certain—pore dear lady."

Mrs. Amorest, wakened from sleep, was at first unaware of the facts behind Mrs. Bloxam's cries. Then she put on her red flannel dressing-gown and hastened with Mrs. Bloxam into the other room.

"I closed 'er eyes, mum. They were starin' open. Pore lamb. She wasn't 'appy and she was a lonely soul. I daresay it's best for 'er that she's gone."

Mrs. Bloxam then standing there in her shabby black hat shed tears. Miss Beringer had, after all, two true mourners.

"I wish now," said Mrs. Amorest, looking down at the poor, tired, worn face, "that I had stayed here last night. I think that she wished me to. When I'd gone to my room I nearly came back. There was something in her eyes that seemed to ask me. At least it was a peaceful way to die, in her sleep, without pain."

Then she saw the dog crouching at the foot of the bed. "Oh, Pip! Poor Pip! What will he do now without his mistress?"

She went up and stroked him. He shivered beneath her hand, looked at her with miserable eyes, but did not move.

Mrs. Amorest looked about the room. "There is that piece of amber on the mantelpiece that she was so fond of. She had it in her hand when I left her. She must have got out of bed to put it up there."

They stood together in silence. At last Mrs. Amorest said, "We must lock the door and send for a doctor. There might have to be an inquest——"

Mrs. Bloxam looked frightened. "Oh lor', mum. And me give evidence?"

"It might be, when there's a sudden death like this. Do you know a good doctor near here?"

"Yes, mum. Dr. Bluett. A very nice gentleman."

"You'd better get him at once, Mrs. Bloxam."

"Yes, mum, I will."

They locked Miss Beringer in. Pip refused to leave the room and he was locked in also.

Back in her own place Mrs. Amorest hurriedly dressed, and as she dressed she blamed herself. She had been hard on poor May Beringer. Had she shown her more sympathy she would have made her happier. Her scorn for weakness and sentimentality in others was her fault, her grievous fault, and all her life it had been so. She could look back over the many years and see occasion after occasion when she had been hard and stern. So she thought. She had been selfish too, filled with alarm about her own little unimportant affairs when this poor woman had been lonely and longing for affection.

But when she was dressed and stood looking from her window at the grey roofs, the creamy sky flecked with shreds of blue, there stole upon her, in spite of herself, a strong apprehension. She was alone now in this house with old Agatha Payne. So sharp was this realisation that she had the impulse to pack her bag instantly and go somewhere else. But where? She would find nowhere else so cheap, and in a boarding-house or lodging-house her liberty and freedom would be threatened, her privacy spied upon, her poverty laughed at. With this came realisation number two—that at this moment she had not a friend in all the world, and that were she to drop down dead as May Beringer had done, with the exception of Mrs. Bloxam's ready tear not a sigh would be breathed, nor a heart show pity.

The sight of May Beringer's pinched white face stranded there, like a derelict boat, on that desolate shore—the picture of that room with its shabby furniture, the grey ashes of the fire, the chill of the air, these things drove at her very heart. She would need her pluck to-day, must stiffen her back, hold up her head as she had never done in all her life before.

The doctor arrived, and after five minutes in May Beringer's room he paid a visit on Mrs. Amorest. He was a little round fat man, pale, and bald like a billiard ball, neat in a grey suit, a little pompous but kindly.

"Excuse me, madam, but your name is Mrs. Amorest, I think, and you are a tenant in this same building."

Mrs. Amorest said that she was, and asked him to sit down. He seemed to like the gentle little lady, was surprised, perhaps, to find such a lady in such a place.

"You were a friend, I think, of the lady who has just died?"

Mrs. Amorest said that she was; not a close friend, Miss Beringer had only recently taken the room.

"Quite so. Quite. And I understand that she was in bed all yesterday. You were with her in the evening?"

"I was," said Mrs. Amorest.

"Did she complain of anything?"

"Yes, of her back and of her heart. She had complained of these to me before."

"Oh yes. Quite so. Had she any trouble, anything to disturb her in any way?"

Mrs. Amorest hesitated. "She was a very nervous woman, easily frightened. She was worried about her money affairs, I think, and her health."

"Exactly. Thank you very much. That's what I supposed."

He got up and made a stiff ceremonial bow, but he smiled and looked kindly.

"Will there have to be an inquest?" Mrs. Amorest asked.

"Well, there may be," Dr. Bluett answered. "It seems a clear case of heart failure. She had been seriously ill for a long time. The slightest worry would be bad for her. She might have dropped down dead any moment in the last ten years, I should say. Had she any relations or friends who ought to be told?"

"Really I don't think there was any one," Mrs. Amorest said. She had a strange feeling that she would like to keep this little billiard ball of a man for a while in her room. He was so friendly. It might be only his professional attitude, of course, but she thought not. She thought that if they pulled their chairs up in front of the fire and had a chat they would become good friends. Strange how long it was since she had had any one to pull up a chair with!

"No one at all?"

"I don't think so. She had one great friend, but she has not heard from her for many years."

"Poor woman. A lonely life." Dr. Bluett gave a little sigh that was as though he were blowing very faintly on a penny whistle. "No one ever came and saw her?"

"I think nobody."

"Dear me. How lonely she must have been." He looked at Mrs. Amorest then as though he were about to say something more personal, but he checked himself.

"Any one else live up at the top here?"

"Yes, there's a Mrs. Payne—a widow."

"Was she a friend of Miss Beringer's?"

"Not really. They met once or twice, I think."

"Well, I may have to disturb her. I don't know. I may not have to bother you again. Good morning."

Mrs. Amorest longed to say, "Oh, do bother me again! Come and see me. I'll give you tea. You don't know what a kindness you'd be doing," but of course she said nothing of the kind.

He bowed beautifully at the door and rolled away down the stairs. When he was gone the silence of the house was insupportable. She did not know what terrors and dismays might not surround her. She would go and buy poor May Beringer some flowers.

As she left the house she fancied that its forbidding dark windows leered after her. She was not given to "dreams and symbols," but she had come to hate the place and felt that it also hated her.

When she arrived in the busy part of the town it was gay enough. The sun was shining and the High Street bustling with people. There was Canon Bentinck-Major talking on the very edge of the curb to that pretty girl, Joan, daughter of Archdeacon Brandon. Mrs. Amorest adored to see pretty young things with plenty of health about them. What she always said was that she could not understand why the Old Lady in the Shoe should be bothered. She only wished that she'd had her chance! Then there was Canon Ryle, the Precentor, smiling and polite to whomsoever. Mrs. Amorest would have liked a smile from him. She admired so greatly the way that he sang the services in the Cathedral, but of course he did not know her so of course he could not smile! Then here was Mrs. Combermere with her dogs and walking-stick and mauve hat with the bright red feather. Now she was greeting the Precentor, and it seemed for a moment that they changed sexes, so masculine and downright was Mrs. Combermere, so smiling and attentive was Canon Ryle!

And then (by this time Mrs. Amorest was almost at the bottom of the High Street), who should turn up the hill from the river but the great Archdeacon Brandon himself! Oh, but Mrs. Amorest did admire him! Some said that he was vain and imperious, but Mrs. Amorest did not think so. She felt that when you were as large and as handsome and as commanding as that, you had a right to be a little vain! He moved with such vitality, such energy, as though he knew just what he intended to do at every step and no one should stop him! She admired him most as he passed from his stall to the Lectern to read the Lesson. How beautiful then he was with his head up, his shoulders back like a general leading his forces into battle! Mrs. Amorest was not sentimental about men, she knew their faults as well as another, but about Archdeacon Brandon she permitted herself some indulgence.

She liked a man to *be* a man, and whatever else Archdeacon Brandon might be, no one could deny him his masculinity!

She had thought that she would buy the

flowers from the gnarled old woman in the market: thither she went. But she had not realised that it was Market Day. The Square was filled with pigs and sheep, dogs and cows. Stout farmers were standing importantly in groups; the booths were all set out with their wares; women were crying their goods, boys shouting, horses neighing. She had not been for many a day in such a regardless multitude, and she stood bewildered with people pushing her on every side, the sun dazzling her eyes. All the world was so gay, and there behind her was that silent house with May Beringer lying dead in it and half-crazy old Agatha Payne mumbling over her fire.

She had a queer impulse to cry like a little girl lost and terrified. She felt again what she had been feeling so often of late—but now with overwhelming force—that nobody wanted her. No one in the High Street had smiled at or recognised her, and now they were jostling and disregarding her as though she were not alive at all! What would happen to her if her few investments descended even lower than they had already gone? She simply would not be able to live at all. She would starve slowly up there in that horrible house and nobody would know and nobody would care. What happened to old ladies when they had no money and no friends? No one cared about old ladies. They cared about old women of the other class. There were homes for them and clubs for them, and societies, and people came and visited them and brought them food and warm clothing. The almshouses nowadays were comfortable and friendly, and all the old women gossiped over the fire. But old ladies were not supposed to go into almshouses; it was not thought that they needed them.

And old ladies were forced to maintain certain appearances. They were expected to look like ladies, to wear nice clothes, and if they did not people laughed at them and thought them odd. The very last thing that Mrs. Amorest wanted was pity or charity, but she did want friends and some one—any one—to care whether she lived or died.

If Mr. Bloxam deceased and Mrs. Bloxam in the course of time grew old there would be no appearances for her to keep up, and people would visit her and her own cronies would come and sit by her fire and gossip. She thought, desolately, standing there, of Brand; but that letter from him had been posted a year ago. For the first time in her history she admitted to herself that he might be dead. It was probable indeed that he was. Why did no one ever think of ladies who were poor and lonely and ill? Every one else in the world was thought of, from the natives in the centre of Africa to the slum children in Seatown. It was true, as Agatha Payne had said, that old people were tiresome and in the way. It was men like Archdeacon Brandon and pretty girls like his daughter Joan whom the world wanted!

This was bad for Lucy Amorest, unlike her in every way. She bit her lips to keep the tears back, and then when a stout farmer knocked past her anger took the place of tears. How rude they were! She refused to be ill-treated by any of them. She was not dead yet, although they might think so. She found her way to the old flower-woman and spent the last penny in her pocket on a large bunch of daffodils. They cheered her a little. They were bright and gay and cheerful and, most certainly, no respecter of persons. To them the rich and the poor, the young and the old, were all alike.

She despised herself, as she went up the High

Street again, for her mood of pusillanimity and cowardice, and, as was her way, spoke to herself inside herself: "Now, Lucy Amorest, you're every bit as good as anybody here. If they look down on you, you look down on them. The game isn't over yet, and there's a good time coming." The daffodils promised her at least that spring was coming, and she was always happy in the spring. As she looked at the blue sky and felt the breeze on her cheek she felt for a moment that she was back again on her beloved northern hills, climbing Cat Bells to turn and see Derwentwater like a silver platter at her feet, looking down upon Thirlmere from Helvellyn, seeing the wind blow the reeds like music on Rydal.

Nevertheless, she must positively beat herself back to Pontippy Square. It was as though something was warning her; never had she found it so hard to cross the cobbles of the Square and pass on up that cold, deserted pavement. No life in any house. The windows dead and deserted. Silence absolute.

She climbed the stairs, hating her cowardice, went to her room and took off her hat, then, with the daffodils in her hand, crossed to May Beringer's door. She unlocked it. The room was cold and bleak. She knelt down beside the bed and tried to pray but, to her horror, no prayer would come.

The house—the stairs, the walls, the grey-faced windows—seemed to push in between her and her prayer. She could not realise God at all; she could not think of May save as motion-less there, passing to corruption with her closed eyes and yellow face. She could think of no prayer at all. She began, "Our Father," and could not remember the words.

She opened her eyes and stared about the room. She thought that May Beringer's left eye opened, winked at her and solemnly closed again. The daffodils that she had laid on the bed looked already faded and dead. There was around her nothing but death and decay.

She got on her feet and stared about her, feeling that in another moment she would sur-render to some horrible blasphemy or impiety.

"Dear Jesus Christ," she said aloud, "do not leave me."

Something moved and she gave a little cry. It was the dog. He came to her, crouched against her dress and looked beseechingly up at her. The relief at his company was so great that she

knelt down there on the floor, took him into her
arms, and pressed his head against her breast.
He did not move except that faintly he licked
her hand. He seemed very feeble, and now
when she moved towards the door, carrying him,
he did not protest.

With a sigh of relief she was back in her
room. The late morning sun was pouring in,
shining on the rose-coloured furniture, the silver
match-box, Brand's photograph. She looked
about her with pleasure. The air was different
here; shabby old room as it was, it was her own
place, filled with her own personality. It knew
her—it had witnessed her hopes and fears and
disappointments. It recognised that she had
tried to brighten it and give it colour and life.
It was grateful. She poked up the fire, put a
cushion in front of it, and laid Pip there. Then
she poured half the milk out of the bottle into
a deep saucer, crumbled up biscuit into it and
tried to persuade him to eat. But he would not
touch it. Little convulsive shudderings passed
over his body. Once and again he raised his
head and stared at the door in acute apprehension. Mrs. Amorest had the strange fancy as
she looked at him that he was oddly like his

departed mistress. The look in his eyes was the same. She had seen just that half-hypnotised stare of alarm in May Beringer's eyes. He would not touch the biscuit and milk, feebly wagged his tail as though he appreciated her kindness, licked her hand again, but would touch nothing. Yet he had not eaten anything since the preceding evening and must be very hungry.

She took her George Herbert and sat down near the fire and tried to be caught into the poems that she so dearly loved. But just as before she could not pray, so now she could not attend to the poetry. She continued to look at the door, and when the dog raised his head and gazed in terrified fashion at the door she also was compelled to look. The conviction slowly came to her that the dog had been witness of something dreadful. He was frightened in reminiscence as well as in anticipation. He had the look in his eyes that she had seen once or twice with human beings, once in the face of a little child who was terrified of her mother, once in a woman who had a drunken husband. What had happened last night? Had May Beringer woken before she died and realised that death was upon her? Had she tried to call for assistance? Why had she

placed the amber piece on the mantelpiece? Had
her heart attack come upon her while she was out
of bed? No, she had been lying peacefully there.
There was no sign of any physical distress. But
how Lucy wished now that she had stayed there
all night. She knew—she saw it all now so
clearly—that May Beringer had longed for her
to stay, had not had courage to ask her. Had she
felt a little more sympathy, shown a little more
understanding, she would have offered to remain
and May Beringer would not, perhaps, have
died. She blamed herself bitterly and vowed
that, for whatever years of life might remain
to her, she would never be scornful of others'
weaknesses nor hard in her judgements. There
was something very humiliating to her in the
thought that after all these years she had not
learnt human charity. She heard the Cathedral
clock dimly strike one, and to change her thoughts
she prepared her frugal meal. She sat at the
table drinking her tea and eating her bread and
cheese. She took from the bookshelf an old
faded volume of the *Cornhill*. It was one that
contained Anthony Trollope's 'Small House at
Allington" with the Millais pictures, and as she
turned the pages she felt comfortable. The old

illustrations with the quaint dresses, the leisurely, happy life, Lily Dale, who knew only the stress of choosing between two lovers, the slow, long afternoons, the quiet evenings, brought back her own youth, happy days, multitudes of friends, eager anticipation of glorious life; all that past seems in retrospect so safe and secure that one wonders why one did not realise its blessings more fully.

She fell asleep in her chair with the volume on her knees; she woke with a start to find the sun low, sinking behind the chimney-pots, and Agatha Payne in the room.

"Agatha!" she cried, starting up, the volume dropping to the floor. "I never heard you come in."

Agatha Payne said nothing. She stood looking out of the window.

"What is it? Do you want anything?"

She slowly turned round. "Why didn't you tell me that May Beringer was dead?" she asked.

Lucy Amorest answered, "Why should I have bothered you? There was nothing more to be done. We had the doctor. She died quietly in her sleep."

"I knew," said Agatha, coming up to the fire. "There was no need to tell me."

"You knew?"

"Yes. She came and told me herself."

Mrs. Amorest said, "What do you mean—she told you?"

"She came this morning and told me. She's never going to leave me again. She's given me the amber, though. She says she doesn't want it any more."

Terror seized Mrs. Amorest. She felt nothing save an urgent passionate desire to escape. She had had enough. She could endure no more.

"Oh, don't tell me!" she cried. "You don't know what you're saying. She's dead. She's gone."

"She hasn't gone," Agatha replied slowly and quietly. "She's here in this house. I killed her body but I haven't got rid of her. She is never going to leave me any more. She says so."

"You killed her?" Mrs. Amorest's voice was a low whisper of horror.

"Yes. I went in last evening and killed her. I didn't mean to, but I frightened her and she died. However, it doesn't matter now, except that I don't want to be left alone with her. She might do me some harm."

Mrs. Amorest rose from her chair and faced her. "Stop that! I won't have it. You don't know what you're saying. You're mad. You don't know what you're saying."

"I know very well what I'm saying. It's true. She came to me this morning as I was sitting in my chair. She stood as close to me as I'm standing to you. She said that I could have the amber and that she would never leave me. But I won't be alone with her. I won't. There's her dog. He knows what I did."

Mrs. Amorest said, "You're ill, Agatha. You must get out of this house and I must too. You don't know what you're saying. Go and lie down in your room. You'll sleep, and when you wake these fancies will have gone."

Agatha moved back to the window. "You're a fool, Lucy. You always were. It's true what I'm telling you. And what's the good of my leaving this house? She'll come with me, I tell you. If I died she'd be with me just the same. But she won't come while you're there. You can keep her away. Well, I've tried you. I'll go now, but I'll come back."

She moved slowly, with her old lurching movement, out of the room.

Is it madness? Is it delusion? Where does this thing begin and end? The transition is so slight and when you are weary, hungry, old, lonely you are fitting prey for any wandering spirit. Agatha Payne—May Beringer's death—these things were real. Real, too, the isolation and the fear. Lucy Amorest had never before in all her life known what fear truly was. She knew it now. She knew it so that it held her where she was; she stood where Agatha Payne had left her as though a spell had been woven about her. Her head was up. She was listening. A tap was dripping in the hall. One—two—three—four and then a number together. She had not known that there *was* a tap in the hall, but now it was the only voice in all that listening, waiting world. Agatha Payne was mad, crazy, off her head. Was she imagining that she had gone into May Beringer's room or had she in reality been there? Had some horrible scene occurred? Poor May Beringer! Oh, poor May Beringer! But if the woman had been there she had not taken the amber. Perhaps it was she who had placed it on the mantelpiece. She had been afraid, it might be, that she would be accused of theft or violence. Had she been sane enough to fear that?

Lucy Amorest's knees were trembling. She sat down upon the bed, leaning forward, her hands clasped, holding herself together. Must she spend another night alone in that place with that woman? But where to go? To a hotel? To Mrs. Bloxam? She shrank from that. There was cowardice in it and especially it seemed to her, in some odd way, that she would be deserting May Beringer all alone there in that chill room. Moreover, she felt that she had no strength. The room was so dark now and the fire so low that she could see nothing, but it needed an immense determination to move to the table and light the candles. When she had lit them they seemed to illuminate the room only in patches. By the door there it was quite dark. It appeared to her now that it must be another woman who must dare to move to the fire, place coal on it, draw her chair to it, find a book. That was what she *should* do, but she was paralysed, standing in the circle of candle-light, listening and counting mechanically to herself the drippings of the tap in the hall. Poor May Beringer!

Had she also heard that tap, lying there in bed and counting? Lucy had despised May's fears, but now she herself had fears as terrible.

She had forgotten the dog. He stirred. He raised his head, then let it fall. That released her from her spell. She went forward and knelt down beside the cushion. She put her arms around him. She heard him sigh, a ghost of a little sigh. He shivered, then lay still.

She knelt for some time with him thus in her arms, then some suspicion flew to her brain. She stroked his head, felt his heart. There was no beat there. He was dead.

She laid him down and drew desperately to her feet. He had died of terror. She knew it as clearly as though in his distress he had whispered it to her before his going. Panic came then crowding in upon her. She could not, she must not stay in this house another moment. She moved, stumbling across the room, found a small handbag in the corner by the chest of drawers, began to pull out handkerchiefs—anything that her hands touched—and to press them into the bag, and at every moment she paused listening. Panic grew upon her. She was afraid to stand in the dark and moved over to the candle-light.

The sight of the dog lying so limply and desolately there moved her to an agony of distress.
She knelt down by him again, stroking him,
speaking to him, doing she knew not what. "Oh,
Pip! I can't bear it. I'm frightened, Pip. I
must get away and I don't know where to go.
I'm so frightened. I'm so frightened! I can't
think. I don't know what I'm to do, I'm all
alone and Agatha's coming back."

She ran to the door thinking that she would
lock it. There was no key. She remembered,
as though it had been a hundred years ago, that
it had not fitted and had been sent to be mended.
She ran back to the fire again. She stood, squeezing her hands together, saying over and over
again: "I don't know where to go! I must get
away! I don't know where to go!"

The door opened. She cried out, "No! No!
You can't come in! You can't come in!"

She saw a great figure that seemed to tower
to the ceiling. She heard a strange voice. The
figure moved forward, and at that, as though at
last her endurance had snapped and she could
bear no more, she put out her hands as though to
shield her face and sank to the floor.

CHAPTER XII

THE HOUSE IS ABANDONED

THE man moved forward into the light. He looked about him in puzzled fashion.

"Is any one here?" Then, as there was no answer, to himself aloud, "There's not a soul about, but the candles are burning——"

He looked over the table and saw the old lady crumpled up on the floor. With a step he was across to her, had her in his arms, was stroking her forehead and crying, "Mother! Mother! It's Brand! Mother! Mother! Old lady——"

He gazed about him distractedly, then heard the dripping of the tap clear through the door that he had left open behind him. In another moment he had a cup in his hand, was in the passage, had filled it and returned.

He picked her up and laid her gently on the bed, took out his handkerchief and damped her forehead, stroking her tiny hands with his big ones, whispering to her.

She stirred; opened her eyes for a moment and closed them again. He heard her murmur something. Then she felt the strong warm pressure of his arms about her, resisted a little, then, still without opening her eyes, settled back against his chest with a little sigh of contentment.

There was something very boyish in the look of distress and anxiety and love that he bent upon her. He was impulsive and forgetful, warm-hearted and generous, but living for the immediate hour, unsubtle, knowing nothing of analysis of character, loyal, quickly angry, nothing mean nor small nor jealous. A little of this you might have guessed from his broad, ugly, good-natured face, his large loose body, the kindliness of his eyes, and something proud in his gaze as he looked down upon her.

He would do anything for her now that he had her in his arms, but that did not mean that he had not gone on, carelessly, happily, without worrying in any way about her for three years or more.

She opened her eyes again and, very slowly, realisation crept into her heart. She started away from him saying confusedly, "What . . . ? Who . . . ? Where am I?" The familiar

things about the room first assured her, then she
saw the body of the dog. "Oh! I remember.
Some one came in!"

She looked up at him, his large, brown, rather
chubby face, the eyes startlingly blue, the hair
receding, but fair and thick—she broke into the
full triumph of her discovery:

"It's Brand! It's Brand! It's Brand!"

She began to laugh hysterically, buried her
head in his rough tweed waistcoat, her hand feeling blindly about his neck, then pulled his head
down to hers, kissing his eyes, his mouth, his
cheeks, his ears, his forehead again and again,
running her fingers through his hair.

"It's Brand! It's Brand! It's Brand!"

"That's better!" He caught her in a great
hug, lifting her right off the bed. Almost he
might have done it with one hand as though she
had been a little grey sparrow. "That's more like
it! I frightened you coming in. It was a silly
thing to do, now I come to think of it, but like
most of the things I do, the thinking came afterwards when it was too late. Now, old lady, let's
have a look at you. What have you been doing
to yourself? You've vanished to nothing at all."

But she could pay no attention to his questions,

she could only say over and over, "It's Brand! It's Brand! It's my son! It's my son!"

"But here," he remonstrated at last, laughing, "we've got to begin to be sensible. What on earth are you doing here anyway? What are you doing in this miserable room, and you look half starved?"

But she could pay no attention to his questions. She gazed into his face as though she were quite crazy, her mouth open, her eyes wide-staring, her hands moving ceaselessly about his body, his hair, his face, his shoulders, his chest, his hands, her fingers touching and holding, withdrawing and clutching again as though she would never be sure of this new reality. And he, looking at her, discovered something of what he had done in leaving her for so long without any word. A passion of love caught him. He put his arms around her, held her close, whispering, "Darling Mother! Darling Mother! I've been a bad neglectful son, but I've got you for keeps now. We will never be separated again."

So they stayed for a while, but Mrs. Amorest was no melting sentimentalist. She drew away from him at last and looking up at him with the old sarcastic smile that he had known so well as a small boy, and had been afraid of, too, said to him quite sharply, "And so at last you've had time to think of your mother? I fancy you're just dropping in for five minutes on your journey somewhere or another. Well, we must be thankful for small mercies, I suppose." This opened the second stage of their proceedings.

"Now, Mother," Brand said, raising his long heavy body from the little creaking bed, "it's about time we began our bit of talk. You come along to this chair. . . . Why, what's the dog?" And then more quickly, "The dog's dead."

"Yes," she said, "he died ten minutes before you came in. That's one thing that had been upsetting me. It's been an awful day." She gave a little shudder. "If you hadn't come——"

"Poor little beggar! Was he your dog, Mother? Had you had him a long time? Look here, we'll put him over there by the window." He picked up both the dog and the cushion and took them to the end of the room.

He settled his mother in the arm-chair, tried one of the other chairs for himself and found it impossibly small, pulled a pillow finally off the bed and settled himself on the floor at her feet.

"Now," he said, looking up at her. (Strange

how quickly an old familiar action can override
the years; the touch of her fingers upon his hair
slew twenty years at one blow.) "We've got to
talk seriously, madame. And, first, I suppose
you would like to know why I came here, frightening you to death without a word beforehand."

"Indeed I would," she said. "I remember
when you were a child of five telling you that
you never thought of others. It's true now as it
was then."

"What a thing to tell a poor child!" he answered. "But scold me. I deserve it. I deserve
it horribly." His voice fell to a graver note:
"I've been a cad, Mother, in this—a perfect cad.
But you'll understand it perhaps a little bit better
—although there's nothing to excuse it, mind—
when I tell you that I have been picturing you
comfortably at Cheltenham with your friends
and that little house with the garden you told me
about, and old Mr. Somebody the parson, and
young Mr. Somebody Else the banker. I thought
you were having no end of a time."

"So I have been," she murmured, "having no
end of a time."

"I haven't had a letter from you there for the
last ever so long. It's true that the last I had

was from this town, but I fancied you were here
on a visit to your cousin or somebody. Then I
myself was always expecting to come home. Did
you ever get a letter I wrote from San Francisco
just about a year ago?"

"Yes, I got it. It was delayed a little, but I
got it."

"That was before I went down to Los Angeles.
I'd had the world's worst luck before that. Things
were always on the point of coming right and
just didn't, and then that illness in San Francisco
topped everything. I ought to have been home a
year and a half ago. Anyway down to Los
Angeles I went, and the luck turned as I hoped
it would, right bang in my direction, has stayed
there ever since, and looks like staying!"

"What were you working at, dear?"

"Oil and land are the things there. Of course,
my little exploits are pretty small at present, but
if the place develops, as it seems to me it's bound
to, I stand to net a mighty pile. Anyway I've
made enough, buying and selling, in the last six
months, to settle you comfortably for the rest of
your days, old lady."

"It never occurred to you, I suppose," she
asked, "that a letter or a telegram to say that

you were coming would have been natural and decent?"

"To tell you the truth, Mother," he burst out, kicking out his long legs towards the fire, "I was all excited with the idea of bursting in upon you. You see, I saw you all set and cosy at Cheltenham, having the vicar in to tea. Many and many a time I pictured it to myself, you sitting there, all cosy, with the curtains drawn and the kettle humming and the cakes and bread and butter on the table and the vicar telling you how good his last sermon was. . . . Oh, you know! And me bursting in upon you like a bomb! Why! I meant to give you the fright of your life—but I didn't think it would be like this. Whatever's been happening? Where's your money gone? You had plenty last time you wrote to me?"

"Plenty!" she smiled rather scornfully into the fire. "That's not exactly the word I'd use. I don't suppose you ever gave a very great deal of thought to the amount—you were never much for details. Don't ask me what has happened to it all. Everything just went down and down. That's all I know. That's all I ever could understand from Mr. Agnew. He used to try and explain technical things to me. I know some of it had to do with railways, but the trains always seemed to me to be full whenever I went near a railway station. But stocks and shares are beyond me, and I've a kind of idea they know I don't like them by the way they run away from me."

He was serious enough by this time. Behind her light tone he was beginning to suspect something of what these last months had been to her.

"How long have you been here?" he asked her sharply. "In this house? These rooms? I'm so late as I am because I missed the train in London. We got into Southampton early this morning. I went off to London the quickest possible, got some money and came on to Cheltenham. I wasn't there half an hour. The post-office told me where you were. They had forwarded a letter, they told me, only a week or so ago. I was lucky enough to catch the train on— and here I am! But how long have you been in these horrible rooms? Tell me."

"Oh, I don't know," she answered, smiling. "Long enough to want to get out of them!"

"Get out of them!" he cried, springing to his feet in a fury. "You shan't stay in them another hour! By God, you shan't."

That was so like him she thought, looking up at him lovingly, and a little sarcastically too. To leave her for so long without inquiry and then to be in a passion of rage at facts to which he had himself contributed. No imagination. He never had had any, and that was strange when his father had had so much. Not like his father at all, with his square thick-set head, his ugly nose, his loose, big-limbed body. She adored him so, as she looked at him, that her hands moved with a little flutter of desire. Then they rested quietly on her lap, and, rather drily, she said:

"And suppose I don't want to move within the next hour? I suppose you've been ordering about people in America to such an extent that you think you can do the same to me. But you've never ordered your mother about yet, and it's not likely that you'll begin now; although I'm seventy and more, I'm not in my grave yet."

How quickly they were recovering their old relations! He found himself already beginning to defer to her, to fear, ever so slightly but nevertheless sufficiently, the accuracy of her sarcasm, and to adore in her, as he had always adored, her independence and courage. It had not been with him, at all, out of sight and out of mind, but it *was* easier for him to realise things and people when they were directly there in front of him. He was realising the old lady more strongly with every moment that passed, and beginning already to wonder how it was that he had managed, for so long, to get on without her.

He was walking about the room looking at the furniture, asking questions:

"But tell me, Mother—you haven't really told me a thing—what made you choose this place? Is there any one else living here? Was that *your* dog? I must know everything."

"You must, must you? I shall tell you only as much as is good for you. As a matter of fact there were three of us up at the top here—two other old ladies beside myself, but poor Miss Beringer died last night of heart failure. And that's her dog."

Brand whistled. "Died, did she? That can't have made things any more cheerful." He looked down at the dog. "Poor beggar—missed his mistress."

"Yes." Lucy Amorest's lip quivered. "Poor May. Oh! I wish she'd lived just for a little while, and now that you're back, you and I. . . . The tears filled her eyes. She turned from him, bending her head in her arm in a passion of sobbing. At once he was with her. His arms were around her. He held her close to him. "Why, mother, what's the matter? Here, old lady, bear up. It's all right now. The trouble's all over. We are going to have the most glorious time. It's all right. It's all right."

"I know . . . I know," she sobbed. "But May. . . . It was my fault. . . . She died of fright, and I might have stayed with her . . . and if you hadn't come I too . . . I was so lonely, and Agatha Payne coming in like that and the money going and no one caring. . . . Oh, Brand, if you hadn't come!"

"I know. I know. I've been a beast, a cad, a brute. I'm so selfish I deserve shooting. I'll never forgive myself for this. The trouble with me is that I never can realise anything unless I see it, but I've learnt a lesson. . . ."

She pulled away from him, smiling, wiping her eyes. "You'll be just the same a month hence—you know you will. But I gave birth to you, so I suppose I'm responsible for you in a kind of a way. I'm not going to think of these last

months ever again.   Although I am seventy-one
I am going to begin life all over again."

"Indeed you are!" he cried.   "And you're going
to begin it by leaving this house within the next
half-hour.   We'll go to the best hotel in Polchester to-night, and to-morrow London!"

"And the first thing I do when I get to the
hotel," she told him, "will be to order a hot-
water bottle.   I wouldn't like to tell you how
I've longed for one all this winter.   You can
have a hot bath when Mrs. Bloxam comes and
lights the heater and all the rest of it, but every
night!   I should think not!"

"Mrs. Bloxam?   Who is she?" Brand asked.

And of all the miraculous and stupendous sur-
prises who should come in at that moment but
Mrs. Bloxam herself!

"Oh, mum," she said, pausing in the doorway
and becoming accustomed to the candlelight after
the deep dark of the stairway, "I couldn't 'elp
coming to see 'ow you was getting on.   I was
just giving Bloxam 'is tea when I said to 'im,
'Bloxam,' I said, 'I'm not 'alf comfortable in my
mind about that poor Mrs. Hamorest with Miss
Bellringer dead beside 'er only a yard or two

away'; and I put on my shawl and come right acrost. If it would make you easier, mum——"

Then she saw a man. "Why, Lord bless us," she cried. "'Oo's that?"

"Come in, Mrs. Bloxam, and meet my son. He's come all the way from America to look after me!"

"Why, what do you make of that!" cried Mrs. Bloxam.

"Brand, this is Mrs. Bloxam, who's been kinder to me than any one else in the world. If it hadn't been for her I don't believe you'd have found your mother alive at all."

Brand gave Mrs. Bloxam so warm a greeting that she was more confused than she had been for many a day. She spoke breathlessly, with deep sighs intermingled, as though she had been running for a mile. "Why, to think of that, and all the way from America; and I always knew 'e was coming, didn't I, mum? When you was losing 'eart I always thought different. 'Why, mum,' I said, 'of course 'e's coming! Do you think a fine upstanding young man like that is goin' to leave 'is very own mother without a word?'—with your mother thinking all matter of dreadful things that you was dead and buried and what all. And only this very evening there was a stranger in Bloxam's tea, which I pointed out to 'im as certain to mean something good. Well, glory be to God! and all the way from America, and you're looking fine and 'ealthy, sir, if I may say so, and the very spitting image of your mother too."

All this was very pleasant, and happiness reigned.

"There's a thing you can do for us, Mrs. Bloxam," Brand said, "and that is get us a cab in about twenty minutes. My mother isn't going to stay in this horrible house another night."

"I'm sure you're right, sir," Mrs. Bloxam said, pulling herself up a little. "But as to 'orrible, I'm not so sure. I've looked after all my ladies to the best of my strength, and it's been none so easy neither with Bloxam uncertain in 'is 'abits and three children, which the youngest, Flossie, is always catching one thing and another, poor worm. I'm sure I've done my best and all them stairs to climb, and two corpses within a six month. Of course, it ain't like a 'otel, and you couldn't expect it to be with one of these old-fashioned 'ouses, and the water 'aving to be 'eated every time there's a bath, which takes hours and hours. All the same, I'm sorry not to 'ave given satisfaction, and me workin' morning and night as you may say, seein' that Bloxam is often not in of a night till three in the mornin'——"

Mrs. Amorest put her arm around Mrs. Bloxam and kissed her on her crimson cheek. "You've been an angel to me, Mrs. Bloxam. My son meant that the house isn't very bright and cheerful, and you know yourself you've often said so."

Happiness was restored. Mrs. Bloxam departed to discover a cab.

"And now—what am I to take and what am I to leave?" Mrs. Amorest cried, looking about the room.

"You're to take nothing but what you'll want for the night and for a few days in London," Brand answered. "We'll have the other things sent on."

"And the silver match-box," said Mrs. Amorest.

"Hullo! who gave you that?"

"My cousin. He left it me in his will."

"Is that all he left you? Stingy beggar!"

"Oh no, Brand. There was no reason why he should leave me anything."

When she had placed a few things in her bag she knew that there was something further that

she must do. She must go in and say good-bye
to Agatha Payne. How she shrank from it!
That other world! She had abandoned it for
ever—oh, surely for ever? To return, even for a
moment, filled her with dismay. But go she
must.

"Wait here for me, Brand," she said, "I must
go across the passage and say good-bye to my
neighbour." She looked at him with longing:

"You won't be gone while I'm away, will
you?"

He hugged her and kissed her. "I won't
move," he assured her.

"I don't trust you," she answered, nodding her
head at him. "If I don't keep you in sight you
may be in America."

She knocked on Agatha Payne's door and
entered.

Within it was as though some spell had been
removed. Always in that room with its close air,
obscurity and old green picture, she had been
conscious of discomfort and apprehension. Now
because all was at last well with her, and she had
passed back again into her own natural kingdom
of light and air and happiness, she saw only an
old woman rocking herself before a fading fire,

a shabby tablecloth scattered with dirty playing-cards, a guttering candle.

But something had happened to Mrs. Payne. As she turned at the sound of the opening door Lucy Amorest could see that she was ill, her cheeks flabby and grey, her eyes wandering and excited. Something of her own fear was returning. Oh, thank God! thank God! that so soon she was escaping.

"Agatha," she said gently, "I've come to say good-bye."

Agatha Payne continued to rock herself as though she had not heard.

"I've come to say good-bye."

"Good-bye? Where are you going?"

"My son's come. Brand. And you said he wouldn't." (She could not keep back that tiny triumph.) "You see I was right after all. He came this evening. We are leaving in a quarter of an hour."

"Don't bother me with your nonsense," Agatha said. "I'll believe in your son when I see him."

"No, but it's true," Lucy Amorest persisted. "He's in my room now. We are going to a hotel for to-night and to London to-morrow."

But the other woman was pursuing her own thoughts.

"Lucy," she said, "come here."

Mrs. Amorest went close to her. Agatha Payne laid a hand on her arm. "Listen! Do you hear anything?"

Lucy listened. "No, nothing," she said.

"Don't you hear any one knocking on the wall?"

"No."

"But you must. Listen again. Do you hear now?"

"No, I don't."

"But it's quite clear. There! Now you can hear it. She's mocking me because I did it to her. She'll be at it all night."

"It's the tap you hear, Agatha—the tap in the passage!"

"You were always a fool." She gripped Mrs. Amorest's arm more tightly. "Now you can hear it. One—two—one—two. . . . I'll beat her at that. I'll beat her."

She lurched to her feet and, leaning forward, knocked on her wall three or four times, pausing between the strokes. She looked round, a grim triumph on her sullen face. "Ah! Now she's stopped! That will keep her quiet for a bit."

Lucy Amorest moved away. "Agatha, there isn't any one. Truly there isn't. You're imagining it." She had a passionate desire now to leave the room. Brand, all the life he brought with him, was receding. He was less real. Agatha Payne was real, and they did not belong to the same worlds, Brand and she. "Agatha, listen. You must listen. I'm going away—now, at once. I must go away."

Agatha Payne turned upon her. "Going away? Oh no, you're not. What! leave me in this house all alone with that Beringer woman! Oh no! You don't! You try it, that's all!"

"But I am. I must. My boy is here."

Agatha moved to the door and set her back to it.

"You don't leave this house—not while I'm alive in it."

Mrs. Amorest felt panic, as she had felt it earlier in the afternoon, slip over her. Where was Brand? Oh, why had she left him? If she called to him he would not hear. What should she do? And she was worn out with the troubles and the joys of that day. No strength was left in her.

"I must go. Please, Agatha. My boy's waiting."

"Your boy!" Agatha Payne answered scornfully. "That's a trick. I know you, Lucy Amorest. You were always a little liar."

"No, but it's true. Come with me into my room and see. You'll feel better in my room. It's staying in here all day by yourself that's so bad for you. Come with me and meet him."

"I won't come," she answered sulkily. "And you'll stay here. We'll stay here all night, the two of us, and when *she* comes she'll have two to deal with."

"But it isn't true, Agatha. She can t touch you. She's dead. She is indeed."

"Dead! I know better than that! You're a little liar, Lucy Amorest. That's what you are!"

"No. Come with me into her room. You can see. Say a prayer with me beside her bed. You won't be frightened any more after that. Come with me."

Her fear had left her. Its place was taken by pity. Something in Agatha Payne's eyes—something lost, wandering, hopelessly lonely—touched her very heart.

She went to her and kissed her.

Agatha Payne moved from the door. "You can go if you like," she said. "I don't want you. You can't help me. She'd never be afraid of you, you feeble little thing!"

"Tell me some way I can help you, something I can do."

"I don't want your help." She went back to her rocking-chair and sat down. "You can't help me! It's between *us*—and I'll beat her yet!"

She sat there, rocking, staring at the fire. She did not look round again, and so Lucy Amorest left her.

Brand was waiting. "The cab's here!" he cried. "Everything's ready. Now, old lady, step out and the sooner we leave *this* place behind us the better!"

Mrs. Bloxam was downstairs, the cab was waiting. Something that Brand placed in Mrs. Bloxam's hand at parting gave her exceeding joy. She shed a number of her happy and facile tears.

The old cab stumbled off across the cobbles. Brand put his arm about his mother and drew her close to him. She had, for a moment, a vision of the house, dead, with blind eyes, and in that upstairs room a woman alone, waiting and listening—no sound anywhere but the dripping of the tap in the hall.

Then her own joy wrapt the rest of the world away from her.

"Oh dear," she murmured, sighing with contented peace. "Is it right, do you think, to be so happy?"

THE END